LIBERATION
MOVEMENTS

Also by Olen Steinhauer

36 Yalta Boulevard
The Confession
The Bridge of Sighs

LIBERATION
MOVEMENTS

OLEN STEINHAUER

ST. MARTIN'S MINOTAUR
NEW YORK

This is a work of fiction. All of the characters, organizations, and events portrayed in this novel are either products of the author's imagination or are used fictitiously.

www.minotaurbooks.com

Library of Congress Cataloging-in-Publication Data

Steinhauer, Olen.
    Liberation movements / Olen Steinhauer.—1st ed.
        p. cm.
    Sequel to: 36 Yalta Boulevard.
    ISBN 13: 978-0-312-33204-4
    ISBN 10: 0-312-33204-1
    1. Police—Europe, Eastern—Fiction.   2. Terrorists—Fiction.   3. Hijacking of aircraft—Fiction.   I. Title.

    PS3619.T4764L53 2006
    813'.6—dc22

                                                                        2006040543

First Edition: August 2006

10 9 8 7 6 5 4 3 2 1

FOR
RH

ACKNOWLEDGEMENTS

•

Far from being an expert on the Armenian genocide, I've taken details from an expert, Peter Balakian, whose book, *The Burning Tigris,* is a sober, comprehensive, and deeply affecting resource on this bleak moment in world history.

The brief chronicle of Soviet investigations into parapsychology is primarily taken from "Amplified Mind Power Research In The Former Soviet Union," a paper by another expert, Martin Ebon. It can be found online.

As this is a work of fiction, I need not mention this, but I will: To my knowledge, no one connected to the Union Church of Istanbul has ever acted to support the cause of World Proletarian Revolution. I thank the church for allowing me to wander inside its lovely chapel.

None of this would have been possible without Slavica, who keeps me warm, happy, and sane.

LIBERATION
MOVEMENTS

PETER

1968

•

"Two days ago—Saturday—we find you in the middle of České Budějovice, walking the main street in a daze. Correct me if I'm wrong, please. You don't have the documents to be in České Budějovice, because you're supposed to be here, in Prague. You're a student of . . ." The Slovak officer bent over the table, the ceiling lamp reflecting off on his hairless scalp as he squinted at his clipboard. "Musicology. A musician?"

"I study theory," said Peter, "but I don't play."

"I see." As the officer stood, his chair scratched the stone floor. "I'm not a mystic, comrade; I can't read minds. So, before sitting down with you here, I ask the faculty; I ask your roommate, this Josef. A feisty one, he is. Almost spits in my face when he tells me you're in Austria by now—safe from the Russian tanks that, as he puts it, *will never crush the flowers of Prague's spring.*" The officer rubbed the edge of his long nose, mustache twitching. "But headstrong Josef is wrong, because by the time of his rash statement you're back in Prague, aren't you? Our esteemed Warsaw Pact comrade-soldiers have brought you and other sundry hooligans back from the Austrian border. Funny, no?"

He blinked twice, waiting, but Peter didn't answer.

"According to your roommate, you left on the twentieth of August, just before the liberating tanks arrived. With your two friends. And now—Josef Kucera tells me—you're all free." The officer tapped a brief rhythm on the tabletop. "Josef tells me that you and your friends will take the plight of Czechoslovakia to the ears of the world. He's very melodramatic, don't you think?"

Ten minutes earlier, this Slovak officer had introduced himself as Comrade Captain Poborsky, but Peter had trouble matching that name to the bald, mustached uniform that squatted beside him and rapped knuckles on the table.

"Yes," Peter told him. "Josef can sometimes be melodramatic."

Captain Poborsky stood again. "Now, I feel relatively sure, at least, of who you are. Peter Husák, student of musicology, amateur rabble-rouser. We have reports on you—nothing deeply troubling, just the occasional demonstration against Russian . . . *occupation,* as you put it. Would you put it that way?"

"I don't know. Maybe."

"Trust me. As a man who works closely with the Russians, I can honestly inform you that their intent here is not occupation, nor is it to *control* us—a country simply cannot control the actions of another. No, their intent is normalization. The Czechoslovak Socialist Republic had already been invaded before the twentieth of August—by ideologues and saboteurs from the West. They just didn't use tanks. And the Warsaw Pact soldiers you see around here, they're volunteers from all the People's Republics, helping us to begin the process of normalization. Nineteen sixty-eight will go down as the year Western expansionism was stopped in its tracks." He tilted his head. "You're a bright kid, I can tell that. You know what I'm talking about."

Poborsky—and this was hardest to believe—*winked*.

"I'm less interested in your minor transgressions—under the sway, of course, of foreign influences—than in the identity of your friends. The ones you left with. I'll find out soon enough, but you might as well tell me now. You see, with those open borders we have no idea who's in or out of the country. It's a bureaucratic nightmare. You can imagine."

Peter affirmed this with a quick nod.

"So?"

Peter focused beyond the bald *Státní bezpečnost,* or simply StB, officer to the corner of the damp room. From there, Poborsky's assistant, a stocky Czech worker with a three-day beard, had stared at Peter during the whole talk. He looked tired in the eyes, because Peter was only one of hundreds he'd had to manhandle from their humid cells down to this cool basement over the last week.

"Peter," said Captain Poborsky. "I don't have all day."

"Toman. My best friend. Toman Samulka."

The state security officer produced a pencil and a notepad from his breast pocket. "Toman's twenty-two as well?"

"Yes."

"And the other friend?"

Saying Toman's name was as simple as revealing your favorite brand of beer. *Budweiser Budvar. Bood-vahr,* almost liking it merely for the rhythm of the name.

"Come on." Captain Poborsky bent so his hands were on his knees and he was looking into Peter's face. "Our prisons are bloated, but that has no effect on how many jokers we send to them."

"Ivana Vogler."

"You're not lying to me, right?"

"Of course not."

"And where are they now?"

"In Austria."

"You're sure of this?"

"I watched them cross over."

"And you?"

"What about me?"

"You're not in Austria," said the captain, "though that's why you left Prague. Your two comrades, Toman and Ivana, they made it. And you—as you've admitted—were there to watch them cross the border. Why did you stay behind?"

"Because . . ." Peter had talked himself into this lie without thinking, and now he'd have to hold on to it. "I don't know why."

"Do you regret your decision?"

"What?"

"Sitting here, now, in this claustrophobic room. Do you regret your decision to remain in the Czechoslovak Socialist Republic?"

Peter raised his head to look at the officer squarely, because this might save him. "No," he said. "I'd never leave my country."

They held him two more days in a hot cell with ten other students who had been picked up in western Czechoslovakia on their way to Austria, but the questions were over. He sat against the stone wall, sweating, and listened to his fellow prisoners, their pronouncements of outrage and their honest but short-lived bursts of fear. Daniel, a Slovak philologist, announced that he was going underground as soon as they let him out. "There'll be partisans, you can bet on it. And I'll join them. Fucking Russians."

The tanks had entered Prague on the night of 20 August, last

Tuesday. The crowds that over that heady spring and summer had filled the streets, forming impromptu committees and rallies to reevaluate socialism in their country, came out once again, now to debate theories of socialist independence with soldiers on the backs of tanks. Dubček had insisted that no one fight the soldiers—he didn't want another Budapest—and so in nearly all cases the arguments were only verbal.

But Peter had seen none of it. As soon as the tanks were sighted in the suburbs, he and Toman and Ivana loaded up their ruck-sacks and packed themselves into the back of a Russian ZIL truck Toman's father had borrowed from his factory. That only took them as far as Tábor, where the engine gave out. Toman's father kissed all their cheeks, wiped away a single tear, and took the train back to Prague. Then they began to walk.

When the prisoners' lectures went on, Peter smiled and nodded but seldom spoke. He had marched with these kinds of people before the tanks arrived, never really understanding the slogans. He understood the language—*socialismu lidskou tvár,* socialism with a human face, was one of his favorites—but politics and economics had never been in his sphere of interest. He'd grown up in this system, and it was because of this system that he'd been able to leave that miserable farm in Encs and begin studies in Prague. Yet he marched, because, more than language or even music, he was interested in Ivana Vogler, girlfriend of his oldest friend, Toman. When she announced that it was time for them all to become politically involved, he learned to march and shout as if he knew what it was all about.

"You're not a spy, are you?"

Peter looked up as Daniel squatted beside him. "What?"

The philologist scratched his beard. "You sit here and listen to everything we say, as if you're collecting information. Where did you resist?"

"I tried to get out. To Austria."

"But you didn't make it?"

"The soldiers caught up with me."

Daniel glanced back at the others in the cell. "Did they get anything out of you? Names?"

"I didn't have any names to give."

"So you're one of us?" He grinned. "A hooligan?"

"I marched," said Peter. "I signed petitions. I suppose that makes me a hooligan, too."

LIBARID

•

It is eleven at night, Tuesday the twenty-second of April, 1975, when Libarid Terzian climbs out of the Trabant in front of Departures. His wife, Zara, and Vahe, his five-year-old boy, help him with the sticky trunk. It's far past his son's bedtime, but he lets Vahe, struggling and tottering but proud, carry his small suitcase to the curb while he kisses Zara. She's teary again, as if she knows something she shouldn't, and for an instant Libarid fears she does know.

"You're going to be exhausted when you land," she says, sniffing.

"Can always depend on the People's Militia choosing the cheapest and most inconvenient transportation."

She gives him a wet smile. No, she knows nothing—this is just the weepiness you grow accustomed to when your wife is a traditional Armenian who's never believed she could be European.

So he kisses her, gives Vahe a hug and a pat on the back. "You're the man of the house now." Vahe likes this at first, but suddenly it seems to frighten him, and he clutches his mother's hand. That quick movement hurts Libarid somewhere in his throat. He wishes he could bring the boy along, but that's just not possible. Not yet.

He clears his throat and waves briefly as they drive off into the blackness, south toward the Capital. Once they're out of sight, he takes a packet of Carpați from his pocket and lights a cigarette. Zara hates it when he smokes.

He doesn't yet feel the freedom but knows it will come, clearing away this melancholy. On the plane, or maybe not until he's lost in the winding back streets of Istanbul, finally loosed from the chains of matrimony.

A taxi pulls up to the curb, and from it emerge a man and a woman. The man is very large, nearly bald, with a small, flat boxer's nose, like the most dangerous lumpenprole he's ever seen. But it's the young woman Libarid has trouble turning away from. Her features are very delicate, and the combination of long black hair with pale blue eyes—he can't stop staring as her companion takes their bags from the trunk and pays the driver.

Libarid steps on his cigarette, opens the glass door to the airport, and smiles. She smiles back as she enters. Her big companion, whose flat face is riveted by acne scars, only frowns.

A sign over the Turkish Airlines desk announces that check-in for the 1:00 A.M. flight to Istanbul isn't until midnight. He has an hour, so he carries his bag to the gift shop, where behind a counter a sixteen-year-old girl sits on a stool, focused on the crossword puzzle in her lap.

"Excuse me," says Libarid.

She says to the crossword, "Yeah?"

"Writing paper?"

Without looking up she reaches to the wall of shelves behind her and grabs a package of fifty sheets, then places it on the counter. "Fifty-four korona."

"A pen, too," he says. "And an envelope."

She sighs and finally looks at him. She drops from her stool and climbs a wooden stepladder to canisters of ballpoint pens. She peers down. "How many?"

"Two pens, one envelope." Then: "No. Two envelopes. I might mess up one."

The girl is not amused by his indecision.

Libarid finds a seat among rows of other travelers in the waiting area. By a high window facing the street, Orthodox Jews—a family—stretch out in silence on their bags, the children dozing; in other chairs sit more crossword players. But what he notices is two rows ahead of him—the beautiful pale-eyed woman and her companion. They don't speak to each other, but the big man sometimes looks around, as if he's protecting her.

Libarid's procrastinating, and he knows it.

So he takes out the writing paper, uncaps the pen, and writes,

My dearest Zara,

No, that's too misleading. He flips to a fresh sheet.

Dear Zara,

He stares at that, repeating the two words until they become a stream of nonsensical syllables. Then he places another clean sheet on top.

Zara—

And isn't sure how to proceed from there.

Two rows up, the woman touches her companion's knee, points to a far corner, and speaks. She must be whispering, because Libarid can't hear a thing. The big man walks with her to the tiled corridor that leads past pay phones to the bathrooms.

Libarid takes the two-toned pamphlet from his bag: INTERPOL INTERNATIONAL CONFERENCE ON CRIME AND COOPERATION IN ISTANBUL, 23–26 April 1975. Emil Brod—Libarid still can't bring himself to call his younger friend "chief"—explained his understanding of the conference. "Brano feels the invitation's largely to seduce us in the East to share more of our resources."

"Why me?"

"You've got a wife and child. You're the safest bet."

"I see."

Emil winked at him. "But as far as you're concerned, it's a vacation interrupted now and then by dull lectures."

He was right. Out of four days of presentations, there's only one that provokes any interest from him: a Swedish delegate, Roland Adelsvärd, on "The Encouragement and Harboring of Terrorists by Various States." Otherwise, it will be a long four days.

Leading, though, to a lifetime of freedom.

When he looks up again the woman is at the end of the tiled corridor, at the pay phones. She speaks into a receiver, nodding, and then places a hand on the wall for support. As if the conversation is very emotional. Then she hangs up, takes a breath, and dials a second number. This call is without emotion, and brief. Once she's done she turns quickly and smiles just as the big man appears, hiking up his pants. He guides her back to their seats, a hand on her elbow.

At midnight, Libarid puts the letter, which hasn't progressed beyond the first word, into his bag and joins a long line at the Turkish Air counter. Halfway up are the woman and her companion. Perhaps because she feels him staring, she turns around fully and settles her pale eyes on him.

He swallows.

She smiles.

PETER

1968

•

Peter and four other students were released without comment on the twenty-eighth of August, 1968, and for a moment the five of them paused, sweating under the low-lying sun in front of the sooty yellow façade of Bartolomějská 9, which had once been a convent and was now a prison. "Does anyone have a cigarette?" Peter asked as he took off the dirty old pinstriped jacket he'd worn for the last week.

A fat young man started to rummage through his pockets.

"Not here," said Daniel, and he led them down the street, then around the corner to Národní, where they walked in silence to the Vltava. Halfway across Legions' Bridge, Sharpshooters' Island was so thick with trees that, from a distance, it looked to Peter as if a forest were growing out of the water. They stopped at the beginning of the bridge, across from the Café Slavia, and the five of them shared three cigarettes, staring at the sluggish Vltava and, upriver, the Charles Bridge and its rows of statues.

"What now?" said the fat one.

"I'm going to find those partisans," said a red-faced student who had, in the jail cell, seemed the most frightened.

"Not me," said Daniel. He stroked a hairy cheek. "I'm going to find my girlfriend and we'll get our papers straight and move out to the provinces. I'm too old for this. I want to raise a family."

"How old are you?" asked Peter.

"Twenty-four."

They all nodded.

Peter thanked the fat student for the cigarette, shook all their hands, and walked slowly northeast from the river, to the Karolinum district, where the university lecture halls were scattered. Some walls still commanded the Russians, in red paint, to go home, while others were coated in fresh layers of white. Soldiers wandered the streets, Kalashnikovs slung over their shoulders, watching him pass. Some were Russian, others Polish or Hungarian, and more races he could not immediately identify. The length and breadth of the Warsaw Pact—excepting, of course, the Romanians, who had refused to take part in the invasion. It was because of people like these—the devoted members of the socialist neighborhood—that his life had changed so radically in the past couple of months. Before, he'd been a mild student examining the fluid structures and semantics of musical forms. There had been nothing hanging over his head, no question of the political landscape, no weight of guilt.

He stopped in the Torpédo, a small, smoky bar just around the corner from Republic Square, on Celetná, and bought a half liter of lukewarm Budvar. He took the beer to a cool corner and settled at a scarred wooden table half in darkness. In other corners large men in dirty workers' coveralls sipped glasses of brandy. Though the bar was nearly full, it was silent, like a film that had lost its sound track.

Peter used a fingernail on the tabletop, scratching out a rough star with bowed lines. He remembered that field outside České Budějovice, the chopped, knee-high cornstalks, and running. Then he looked up at the sound of boots clattering up the steps outside. The door opened.

The soldier was large, with a round, generous face, and his fatigue-green jacket put Peter's grimy pinstripes to shame. A rifle hung from his shoulder. In the doorway he judged the situation, then stepped over to the bar and asked for a beer.

The bartender got to it immediately.

The soldier leaned back against the counter and looked over the crowd, casually, as if he were not part of an invading army. Peter didn't meet his eyes at first, staring instead at his scratched star, but then raised his head. The soldier noticed, smiled, and turned to pay for the beer. He wandered with his glass over to Peter's table.

"Is okay?" he said in stilted Czech.

Peter shrugged; the soldier sat down and sipped his beer. Then he pulled his lips tight over his teeth.

"Mmm. Is good. That." He pointed at Peter's glass. "You like, too?"

The soldier's cheeks, pinked by the cold outside, were chubby; his eyes were wet. He had a face not unlike Peter's but without a student's gauntness; the invader was well fed. Peter spoke in the soldier's language: "You don't have to speak Czech. I grew up in Encs, just on our side of the border."

The soldier laughed. "That's a relief! Try starting conversations when you don't know how to speak. No one wants to talk to me."

"It's not because of the language."

The soldier considered that. "You get conscripted into the army, and six months later you find yourself in Prague. But you're

as far from a tourist as you can be. And the whole city hates you."
He shrugged. "It's the injustice of the world."

Peter agreed.

"Listen, I'm Stanislav. Stanislav Klym. I'm only here two more
days—my captain gave me my discharge papers today—and I
want to celebrate. Can you afford to be seen with me?"

"Are you buying?"

Stanislav winked. "I'm buying."

So Peter let the foreign soldier buy him Budweiser Budvar; and
while Peter said little, Stanislav spoke like a nostalgic old man, describing his life back in his hometown, his plans for becoming an
engineer, and his girlfriend, Katja Uher.

"She's young—seventeen—but I've known her most of my life.
We're from the same village, Pácin. Once I get back we're going to
move into my apartment in the Capital. I can absolutely not wait."

"You have your own apartment?"

"Used to be my grandfather's. When he died, my grandmother
moved back to Pácin so I could take it over. Of course, as soon as
she gave me the keys I was packed off to the army, so I haven't enjoyed it yet." He grabbed his pocket, making a sound like loose
change. "I always keep them with me, just to remind me what I've
got to go back to. And this," he said, reaching into another
pocket. He took out a crisp photograph and placed it on the
table: a girl with dark eyes and a handsomely bent nose inside a
bob of blond hair. "She's a smart one, my Kati. I think she'll be a
mathematician. Numbers—she's got them all figured out."

"I'm no good with numbers," said Peter, lifting the snapshot
and staring at the face.

"You're also uglier than she is." Stanislav raised his glass. "To
my Katja's unbearable beauty."

They both drank.

"They give you a good coat," said Peter.

Stanislav rapped the table with his knuckles. "Socialist quality, one hundred percent!" He put the photograph away. "Lots of pockets—I can fit my whole life in them. Apartment keys, documents, my girl. I even carry this."

From his belt, Stanislav unhooked a knife and set it on the table. The leather sheath was worn and old, the burned-in design of a hawk with folded wings just visible. "Belonged to my grandfather. My father presented it to me when I got sent here. We drank brandy to celebrate. The old man even cried."

"Why did he cry?"

"You know. Sentimentality. Fathers get that way over their sons."

Peter tried to judge whether this was a joke. He could not remember his own father crying for him. There had been tears, but only for the animals that died on the farm, placing his family that much closer to starvation. And the tears were always tamed by alcohol, which gave his father the strength to rage—at his whore of a wife, at his useless son. *You're a humiliation for me—you know that? Get your fucking education, what do I care? A goddamned humiliation.*

"Sure," said Peter, lifting the knife. He unsheathed it and found his own face in the reflection of the clean blade. "Sentimental fathers."

As they talked, Peter noticed the bar clearing out. The men would stare at one another across their tables, then at Stanislav's back and the Kalashnikov he'd propped against the table. Then they would leave. After a couple of hours, Peter and the soldier were the only customers, and Stanislav looked over his shoulder. "Yeah," he said. "This keeps happening."

"Where are your friends?"

"Eh?"

"You're out here celebrating, but you're alone. Where are the other soldiers from your regiment?"

Stanislav scratched his neck under his collar. "It's a funny thing. They stick us in mixed regiments—internationalism or something like that—so I'm surrounded by Polacks and Bulgars and Ukris, and we all communicate in what little Russian we know. There was only one other guy from home, and he . . . well, he was killed last week, over at the radio station. I don't know." He waved for another round of drinks. "It's all right, they don't want to mix with me either. So I figure it's best to celebrate on my own. Or with you. No?"

"And if I hadn't come along?"

He reached into yet another pocket and tugged out a wrinkled envelope. "I'd reread Katja's letters. Again and again."

LIBARID

·

Sitting at Gate 7 among yawning travelers, Libarid chain-smokes the rest of his Carpați and writes only five sentences to his wife:

> For someone who weeps so much, it's strange to me how deeply you hate sentimentality. But you do. You call it "fake emotions." So I won't pad this with sentimentality. I'm leaving you.

Then he stares through the large windows at the midnight darkness where lights seemingly unattached to planes take off and land. He wonders, again, about the mechanics of later getting Vahe out, and for the first time realizes he's been fooling himself: He'll never see his son again.

On his way down the corridor to the duty-free shop, he spots the woman again. She's speaking with a tall, mustached man who's holding a black briefcase and sweating. He's visibly nervous, though the woman is calm, her smile serene.

In the shop he finds one other customer—the woman's big

companion—also buying cigarettes. The oaf smokes Moskwa-Volga. He ignores Libarid as he leaves.

A little before one o'clock, they board, and Libarid takes his window seat in the twentieth row. He's relieved, as they all are, to finally be on the plane. Across the aisle from him, the nervous mustached man with the briefcase is sitting down. Then Libarid hears a voice.

"This is me."

It's the woman, settling into the seat next to him.

Her companion is nearer the front of the plane, unaware that she's passed him, but then he figures it out. He pushes through people to get back to her. Without speaking, she shows him her boarding pass. The man looks dumbly up at the seat numbers, then holds out his own boarding pass to Libarid. He says, "I need to switch seats with you." He has the clotted voice of a deaf person.

"I'm comfortable here," says Libarid.

The man leans closer, forcing the woman back into her seat. He could break most of the people on the plane in half. "I insist."

"So do I," says Libarid.

The man places a big hand on Libarid's headrest. "Don't be a nuisance, comrade. Not unless you want the Ministry for State Security on you. I'm here to protect this woman."

Libarid pauses, unsure, but then the woman touches his thigh with the side of her hand, just briefly, and it strengthens him. He says, "I'm a lieutenant in the People's Militia. That tough-guy talk may work for the peasants you usually run into, but not with me."

The man recoils slightly, maybe surprised, then looks at the woman. "I'll be seven seats up."

"I know," she says.

Once he's gone, Libarid, flushed, asks if he's really from Yalta Boulevard.

"Don't worry about him," she says.

Libarid stops worrying. "He's protecting you?"

"Protecting, watching—it's all the same, isn't it?"

Libarid points out that it's strange for the Ministry to send a deaf man to watch over someone; it doesn't make much sense. The woman smiles, her pale eyes slits, and eludes him with a question. "When did the Ministry ever make sense?"

The lights dim, and they take off. She closes her eyes as Libarid takes the opportunity to look closely at her face. He lights another cigarette and feels the old pull of his checkered youth, when he had many women, before he settled down. He wonders if he'll return to that checkered youth.

Probably.

Though he's leaving his family, something in him believes it's immoral to try anything yet. It's too soon. It would prove with scientific accuracy that he never had any respect for his wife, his marriage, or his family in the first place.

So Libarid peers past her to the nervous man. He's worse now that the vibrating plane is airborne: sweaty and pale, wiping his mustache and staring at a book he's obviously not reading. Libarid notices that on the cover are the squiggly characters of his own native language. The Bible. Libarid leans over the dozing woman and gives a high whisper. "*Parev!*"

The man looks up at him, almost terrified.

"Nice to see another Armenian face," says Libarid. "And don't worry. The pilot may be a Turk, but he knows what he's doing."

The man nods, a little stunned. "*Aayo*—yes, I'm sure he does."

Then he goes back to his Bible, and Libarid looks out the window at blackness.

Eyes still shut, the woman says, "He's not afraid of flying. He's afraid of dying. Everyone's afraid of that."

Libarid turns to her. "Just trying to help him out."

"It's ironic."

"What is?"

She doesn't answer. She opens her eyes. "Are you happy?"

"That's a strange question."

"You're married. You have a son. I'm just wondering if that makes you happy."

"Sure."

"Then why are you leaving them?"

Libarid stares a moment into her pale blue eyes, which remain steady, watching as he tries to comprehend this. The letter. She must have seen the letter. While he was buying cigarettes, she must have gone through his bag. But Libarid has been a militiaman for over thirty years. He knows not to give her the reaction she wants. He clears his throat. "What makes you think I have a wife and son?"

"It's the way you walk," she says. "Married men have a certain confidence that's not for show. Single men who look confident do it for show."

"And a son?"

She raises her shoulders. "Again, the walk. Biologically, you've accomplished what you were born to do. You have someone to carry on your name. As for you leaving them . . . well, you're freeing yourself from the guilt of affairs by leaving. It's obvious that if I gave you the chance, you'd fuck me in a second."

"What a mouth."

She smiles, and it seems like an honest smile, as if she's been fond of Libarid for a very long time. She settles her head in the seat again.

"So who are you?" he asks.

"Me? I'm nobody. But my name is Zrinka."

"I'm Libarid."

"I know."

He ignores this. "Why are you going to Istanbul?"

"The Interpol conference, just like you."

"You're a militiawoman?"

"Hardly." Zrinka pauses. "But I have a feeling I won't make it to the conference."

"Oh, we'll both make it. Your friend will make sure. I've got a couple friends, too, waiting for me. My *chap*erones."

"Don't worry," she says. "You'll lose them. I *know* it."

"You think you know everything."

"I have a knack for suppositions. For example, in about ten seconds that man next to us—his name is Emin Kazanjian—is going to walk to the toilet. But he won't make it to the toilet."

"What are you talking about?"

"Just watch."

Zrinka closes her eyes as if there's no need to see, and Libarid looks over just as the nervous man sets aside his Bible and gingerly takes his briefcase from under the seat. He carries it slowly toward the bathroom in the front of the plane. Just before he reaches it, though, he stops and turns around, looking at faces. At that moment, three men, spread throughout the plane, get up as well and move to the aisles.

Libarid, understanding now, allows himself a curse: "Oh shit."

That's when Emin Kazanjian shouts.

"Your attention, everyone! This plane is being taken over by the Army of the Liberation of Armenia!"

Everyone gasps. The three other men pull out handguns.

The hijacker raises his briefcase. "There's a bomb in the baggage compartment, and I'm holding the detonator. So no one move!"

Despite all this activity, what Libarid notices is that Zrinka's eyes are still closed. Then she whispers:

"See what I told you?"

GAVRA

•

Captain Gavra Noukas blinked a few times in the early morning darkness. Someone was banging on his door. Face in the pillow, he first saw the dirty hotel glass on the bedside table and caught the rough scent of so many crushed cigarettes. The banging continued. He raised his head, but slowly because of the hangover. "Wait!" he called.

From the other side of the door came the old man's voice. "We're late, Gavra. I told you before. Four o'clock."

Beside him in the small bed, the young, handsome Turk from last night shifted, muttering in English, "What the hell is that?"

"Quiet." Gavra held a finger to his lips and slipped into his underwear. He opened the door a couple of inches. In the bright corridor stood a short, graying old man with three moles on his cheek. "I'll be out in a minute, Comrade Colonel."

The old man's expression betrayed none of his feelings. "Get some clothes on. Now. I'll be in the car."

He closed the door and rubbed a hand through his hair. As the young man sat up, the sheets fell from his thin, pale chest, revealing the long white scar Gavra had discovered last night while undressing him. At the time he'd hardly noticed it. "Who the fuck's that?" the Turk insisted.

"I have to go to work," said Gavra. "Which means you have to go as well."

"At four o'clock in the morning?" The young man pouted with a certain effeminacy and aura of desperation that Gavra found revolting. "We can't even have a coffee together?"

Gavra threw him his underwear.

Quietly, the young man said, "It's a long walk home."

So Gavra tossed some Turkish lira on the bed as well. "Come on, let's move."

He might have been kinder to the young man, but the fact was that Gavra couldn't remember his name.

Colonel Brano Sev leaned against the rented blue Renault just down the narrow, cobbled street from the Hotel Erboy, smoking. When he saw Gavra step out of the lobby into the warm early dawn, he climbed in and revved the engine.

As the car lurched and trembled over stones, he said, "This isn't the kind of behavior I expect, Gavra."

"I should have set my alarm."

Brano shook his head, and Gavra noticed he was looking slightly different. Over the last year of Gavra's apprenticeship, largely at his urging, Brano had gradually acquiesced to sideburns. Gray and thick. Brano said, "I mean picking up girls, Gavra. There was someone else in your bed. I could see her moving."

Gavra opened his mouth but then thought better of it.

"You've got the stupidity of youth. If you want to make it anywhere in the Ministry, you have to grow up."

Gavra told him he understood, then looked out the window

down the length of Sultanahmet Park to the domes and minarets of the Blue Mosque topped by sunlight and proved that he didn't understand at all by saying, "But this isn't the most sensitive of jobs. All we're doing is picking him up from the airport."

Brano Sev didn't answer at first. He took a long breath, the kind he took when gathering patience. The Comrade Lieutenant General, a big man who tended to speak in fraternal shouts, once pulled Gavra aside and explained that Brano had never wanted to take on a 29-year-old pupil. *But don't worry,* the head of the Ministry told him, *he's an old man who knows much more than he's able to do, and we've made the decision for him.*

Brano Sev exhaled, glanced in the rearview, and spoke slowly. "Just suppose that we arrived late. Libarid Terzian's plane has let him off and he's had a half hour to stand around in the arrivals lounge, waiting for us."

"He can take care of himself, Comrade Sev."

"I'm not disputing that," said Brano. "He's a homicide inspector; he knows how to protect himself. But let's say he's had a half hour to consider his options. Let's say he decided he didn't want to return home. Do you know how simple it is to lose yourself in Istanbul?"

"But he has a family. That's why he was chosen for the conference. *That's* why he was issued an external passport."

"How do you know he loves his family?"

For some reason, Gavra had never considered that possibility.

"Twenty years ago," Brano explained, "Comrade Terzian embarked on a rather reckless affair with another militiaman's wife. Though it didn't last, he has admitted more than once that this woman was the love of his life. But, since she was no longer available—she decided to stay with her husband—he married

Zara Sasuni and has built a life he probably never really desired. It wouldn't be so strange if he wanted to leave this life."

Brano paused to let the story sink in.

"You see, Gavra, no matter how many electric ears we place, no matter how many feet of film we have on them, we never know what's going on. Up here." He tapped his temple and turned onto Kennedy Caddesi. Off to the left, the Sea of Marmara opened up, sprinkled with freighters.

Atatürk International Airport was a long, low building west of Istanbul, in a barren, burnt-grass corner of Yesilköy. Brano parked in the middle of the lot, and as Gavra followed him inside, he noticed how the old man glanced around in an unconscious fashion, and how he didn't even register the man with a cart of drinks who sang his price to them. In the arrivals lounge, Brano scanned the board marking planes and times. Gavra peered over his shoulder. "See? It's late."

The board didn't say how late Turkish Air Flight 54 was, so Brano spoke with a girl at the information desk while Gavra lit a cigarette. Families wandered and settled heavily on chairs, waiting for the delayed plane. Brano returned, running his tongue behind his lips. "She says they don't know how long."

"Here, have a cigarette."

"You see that man over there?"

Gavra followed his gaze to the corner. Beside a potted mullein stood a small man in his late twenties with a wire-thin mustache out of a comic book. "What about him?"

"His name's Ludvík Mas. What's he doing here?"

"Why don't you go ask him?"

Brano gave him a look he'd seen too many times on this trip already.

Gavra bought two coffees from the singing vendor and handed one to Brano. Ludvík Mas, still in the corner, looked at his watch. "He's waiting for the same flight," Gavra pointed out.

Brano ignored his perceptiveness. "Come on."

They walked back to the information desk, where a policeman had joined the clerk.

"Hello," Brano said in English. "I'm waiting for Flight 54."

"I told you before," the clerk said, her face stern. "You'll receive information on that when everyone else does."

Brano took a red Interior Ministry certificate out of his pocket and handed it over. She squinted at the strange language, while the policeman frowned over her shoulder. "I'm a government official."

"Not the Turkish government," said the policeman.

As Brano stared at the smirking officer, Gavra sensed the cool, hard anger he'd felt only a few times over the last year of his apprenticeship. Brano said, "Are you interested in causing an international incident?"

The policeman didn't answer.

"Because when I shoot you, my diplomatic immunity will allow me to walk out of here a free man."

As the policeman lifted a telephone and began to dial, Brano returned to his native language and said to Gavra, "Keep an eye on Ludvík Mas while I find out what's going on."

When Brano sauntered off down the corridor with the policeman, Gavra lit another cigarette and leaned on a column. Beyond Ludvík

Mas stood a young security guard with a machine gun hanging from his shoulder. Ludvík had that harried, claustrophobic look of men from their country, with his self-conscious mustache, disorganized sideburns, and too-tight suit, while the guard's handsome face suggested—to Gavra, at least—relaxation and self-confidence: a few days' beard, cap perched back on his head. Even his Uzi seemed a fashion accessory. As he watched the guard, Gavra felt the relaxation that Istanbul always brought him. Beautiful boys and a hot, clear sun that kept his skin tingling. The mosques appealed to his amateur aestheticism, mesmeric prayer-songs filled the city five times a day, and the expanse of the Bosphorus dividing Europe from Asia made his country's stretch of the Tisa look like an open sewer. Istanbul was so different from life in the Capital, where clouds darkened the sky and the men were . . .

Gavra rubbed his nose.

Where the men were closed to new experiences.

That was when Gavra finally comprehended Brano's words. Because, love for one's family or not, who would not choose to shake loose of the Capital and stay, indefinitely, in this paradise?

Then Ludvík Mas left the mullein plant to use one of three pay phones along the opposite wall.

Gavra sipped his coffee as he followed, watching Mas nod into the telephone and bite his lip between words. He reached the next phone and picked it up. Mas was saying, "Of course it's irregular. That's what I'm telling you."

Gavra slipped in a coin and began to dial a random number.

"Okay. But patience isn't easy. Yes. Yes."

Mas hung up and walked back to his corner.

"Who are you calling?" It was Brano.

"I was listening to Mas's conversation."

Brano, blinking rapidly, shook his head. "Forget that for now. Come with me."

He followed the colonel down a busy corridor to a door marked GÜVENLIK—security—beside which stood another handsome guard wearing a tall cap. Gavra gave him a smile he didn't return.

The airport security office was small and dark, lit almost solely by the blue haze of video monitors and the glow of five cigarettes held by five sweating men. The scent of Turkish tobacco, which last night at the club had seemed so intoxicating, now made him want to flee.

"This is my associate, Gavra Noukas," Brano said in English. "Nothing is to be kept from him."

It was an introduction he appreciated. Gavra nodded at each man, but none introduced himself. A fat Turk sitting in front of the monitors, said, "What to tell? There is no more plane. It blow up over Bulgaria."

Gavra touched the back of an empty chair to steady himself. "What?"

"The pilot, he reports they are hijacked. So we talk to the hijackers—Armenians, members of . . . of the what?"

"Army of the Liberation of Armenia," said another man.

"Who are they?" Gavra asked.

The fat man shrugged. "Who knows? Just more dis . . . disaffected Armenians what think his empty bank account is the fault of Turkey. We talk to them, then lose contact. Then the plane, it disappear from the radar."

"You're sure it exploded? It didn't go down?"

Brano explained. "The Bulgarians saw it. Sofia Airport reported the fireball."

"Before we can answer the demands," said the fat man.

Gavra turned the empty chair around and sank into it. "Then why did they hijack the plane?"

The fat man shook his head. "You think I know, kid?"

"You said you have a recording?" asked Brano.

The fat man nodded. "They bring the equipment right now. But it's no help. None. Probably they just wire the bomb all wrong. Fucking Armenians."

Brano turned to Gavra. "I want you to watch him, Ludvík Mas. Maybe he has nothing to do with this, but if he leaves, you follow. Do *not* make contact, only follow. Here are the car keys. You understand?"

"Okay," Gavra said. "But Libarid, wasn't he Ar—"

"Now," said Brano.

PETER

1968
•

It was seven by the time he left Private Stanislav Klym and, a little drunk, began tracing his steps back through the darkening university district. He was surprised by how unchanged it looked. He'd expected crumbled buildings and commons areas turned into impromptu graveyards, but Prague was much as it had been before he left, the few people he saw only looking a little more exhausted.

He caught a half-empty tram, held onto the leather strap, and, as he swung back and forth, wondered if he hated, or if he should hate, Stanislav Klym. There was something that gnawed at him about the man, but it wasn't hatred. Despite the invasion, and despite what had happened outside České Budějovice, he never felt the urge to spit in any soldier's face. They were boys just as he was a boy, taken from their homes and stuck in a city where, like Stanislav, they'd rather be tourists.

He wasn't upset with Stanislav because of his uniform but because of what the man had. Stanislav was happy; he had a life back home he was eager to return to. Whereas Peter Husák was returning to nothing.

In the Tenth District he got out and walked up Pod Stanicí to the Hostivař dormitory, which was decorated by a painted proclamation: AN ELEPHANT CANNOT SWALLOW A HEDGEHOG. He nodded at the young men who stood at the front door as if they were guarding the place. Inside, a thin, spectacled political science student ran up to him. "Jesus, what are you doing here?"

"I didn't make it, Jan."

Jan gripped his shoulders and squeezed as tight as his weak fingers could manage. "Christ. Peter—"

"I'm really tired. Can we talk later?"

"Yes, yes. Of course." Jan patted his back. "I'm glad you're all right. Josef's up there now."

He took the stairs to the second floor and paused in the empty corridor. The window at the far end was broken, and a cool evening breeze swept through. He took a breath and knocked on the door marked 305.

"Yeah?"

On one of the two cots, his roommate, Josef, lay with a book propped on his chest. Then he dropped it and was on his feet, his small, dark face twisting. "What happened?"

"They caught me," he said as he dropped into his own cot. "Near České Budějovice."

"Where's Toman?"

Peter shook his head. "Toman and Ivana weren't caught."

"They made it?"

"I assume so."

Josef paced a moment, as if this news opened a whole new world to him. Then he stopped. "But you're all right, Peter? They didn't hurt you."

Peter stretched out and intertwined his fingers behind his head. "Just questions."

"And?"

"And what?"

"Did you give them anything?"

Josef had never wanted to bring Peter in on the marches in the first place. *He's got no political conviction,* Josef had told Toman. Peter shrugged. "I don't know enough to tell them anything. You never let me know."

The pacing began again. "You see why now? If they'd gotten names out of you, there'd be hundreds more dead."

"Yes, Josef."

"They were around here, you know. Some bald bastard. Asking questions."

"Yes, I know."

"But at least Ivana and Toman made it. They'll let the Americans know the truth." He finally sat on his cot and clasped a knee. He sniffed. "Say, Peter . . . are you drunk?"

"A soldier bought me drinks."

"One of ours?"

Peter shook his head.

"And you accepted his drinks?"

"I needed them. If you'd ever been in prison, you'd know." He closed his eyes. "All he wanted was to tell me about his girlfriend."

GAVRA

•

Back in the arrivals lounge, Gavra lit another cigarette. His hand didn't shake, but it seemed that it should. A plane had exploded. His stomach felt like it was working on a stone.

Claustrophobic Ludvík Mas was still by the mullein, trying unsuccessfully to look patient. Gavra scanned the other faces in the crowd, old women and young men and whole families. There was no concern in their sweating faces, only frustration. Some approached the information desk, and the girl did a good job with her smiles and sympathetic shakes of the head, as if she really didn't know what was going on. Maybe she didn't.

Ludvík Mas checked his watch. He confirmed it with a clock on the wall—6:48 in the morning—then walked over to the telephones. Gavra joined him, two down.

". . . nothing, that's what I'm telling you. And they're not saying anything."

Gavra tapped cigarette ash on the floor and began to dial.

"Who told you that? . . . I would have noticed something, some activity . . . Okay. Yes, comrade, you're right. It does appear she didn't play along."

Then Mas hung up and walked out of the airport.

The morning sun was hotter than Gavra expected, beating down as he slipped on his sunglasses and followed Mas across the parking lot to where he got into a rented beige Mercedes. Gavra half-jogged to his Renault.

On the drive back into Istanbul, he convinced himself that Ludvík Mas was behind the hijacking. There was no reason to believe this, but he believed it just the same, and he was self-aware enough to know why. He was too attached to surfaces, always falling victim to that word Brano Sev enjoyed harping on—sentimentality. *It is,* Brano had told him numerous times, *the demise of all good operatives, resulting in the most fatalities. But you're young. You just don't understand yet.*

And that, as Gavra well knew, was true.

It had been true the previous winter, back in the Capital, when a young woman named Dora was discovered taking photographs of military documents at her office and delivering them to her lover, a West German with diplomatic papers. Gavra had been alone on that case—Brano was on one of his many Vienna trips—and had decided that she was, in the end, apolitical. She was simply in love, and thus capable of immense stupidity. So he didn't bring her in. The next day, Dora flew to Bonn with her lover and was promoted to major in the West German secret police, the BND.

The Mercedes maintained an even clip, following signs to Beyoğlu, yet sometimes Gavra had trouble keeping up. He swept around two car accidents, neither serious but both surrounded by small Turks shouting at one another and waving hands in the air.

Finally, after driving up Atatürk Bulvari and across Atatürk Bridge, spanning the Golden Horn, then rising toward the Galata Tower, Mas stopped at a surprising place: the splendorous cube of the Hotel Pera Palas, where he handed his car keys to a doorman and strolled inside. Gavra parked a little farther down the narrow street, then jogged back, narrowly avoiding an accident.

When he reached the ornate foyer, with Ottoman columns and a wall of coral marble, Mas was to the left, at the front desk, taking his key from a smiling clerk. Then he jogged up a few stairs and entered the century-old elevator.

For the next half hour, Gavra waited in the lounge with a copy of the *International Herald Tribune,* reading dismal editorials on Pol Pot's recent proclamation of the "Democratic Republic of Kampuchea" in Cambodia before drifting to thoughts of Armenians.

Being at the top of his class in the Ministry academy, he had a strong grasp of history. He knew that, despite Turkish claims to the contrary, a series of forced movements took place in the early part of the century, coming to a head in 1915, when the ruling group known as the Young Turks took it upon themselves to rid their country of Armenian Christians while the Great War diverted the rest of the world's attention. The expulsion was carried out so systematically that no one could reasonably deny that orders from above set it in motion.

The Turkish military was first purged of Armenian soldiers, often by group execution. Then cities and villages were taken over by newly purified Turkish troops, who killed Armenian men and forced the remaining women and children into overcrowded trains that spilled them into the desert, or sent them on death marches, where they died of starvation and disease under the summer sun. Reports from American and German officials at the time noted that the roads were lined and rivers choked with the rotting bodies of these ill-fated people. Later, according to a questionable

American journalist, Adolf Hitler would tell his generals, *Who, after all, speaks today of the annihilation of the Armenians?*

Gavra believed most complex disputes to be hopeless, and this one was no exception.

Brano had often wondered aloud about his pupil's innate pessimism when it came to international affairs. *Then why are you working for the Ministry? If you don't believe some sort of good can come from what we do, then why are you doing it?*

Gavra had been recruited straight out of high school, by a man in his village he knew his father despised. He joined in order to make his father suffer for a childhood of humiliations. Even though it had begun in anger, over the years Gavra had found security in the shell of the Ministry that he nonetheless treated with suspicion. So why did he remain?

Not even he knew the answer.

He closed the newspaper and tried to recall Libarid Terzian. He didn't know Libarid that well—only through his file and a few casual conversations—but for the last year they had sat at desks in the same room, and Gavra couldn't help but mourn him in some way. Libarid and his late mother had been part of that stream of Armenian refugees fleeing the terror today's hijackers had sought to revenge.

Ludvík Mas returned to the front desk carrying a small suitcase. He handed over his key, paid his bill, then walked past his shadow and through the front door.

On Atatürk Bulvari, passing another accident, he considered running Mas off the road. This man, who no doubt brought down a plane full of innocents, was probably going home. It was one thing in this world that Gavra could point at and, without hesitation, call *wrong*.

He sped up, halving the distance.

Once they reached the airport, he and Brano would have to go through the Turks in order to do anything, but here on the open road, Gavra could take care of Mas himself. It was an appealing option.

Like during other moments of decision, though, Gavra flustered as the old man's orders came back to him: *Do* not *make contact, only follow.*

"Shit," he muttered.

Gavra loosened his grip on the wheel and let Mas pull farther ahead. He turned on the radio for comfort, and half-listened to pop music with lilting Arabic tones as they left town again. He tapped his finger on the steering wheel, trying to whistle with the tune, but found that it was always slightly different than he expected; it was unpredictable.

When he thought he'd finally gotten the melody down, Mas took the exit for Atatürk International Airport.

Gavra switched off the radio.

Mas carried his suitcase inside. He returned his keys to a car rental desk, then went to the small TisAir desk in the departures area. He bought a ticket and smiled at the heavyset Turkish woman who sold it to him, then walked through the security check to the gates.

Gavra approached the TisAir desk with his most winning smile. "Excuse me. I know you're going to think this is rude, but you have the most beautiful eyes I've ever seen."

She blushed. "Well . . . well, thank you."

"I bet this is an interesting job."

She snorted. "I *wish.*"

"People going all over the world, and you're the one who puts them on the path. That's not so bad."

"But I stay here."

"That may be true, but you meet the world through this desk. Like that man who just left. Where was he going?"

In the arrivals lounge, the earlier frustration had become misery. Women wept beside the mullein plant, and men shouted as if they'd just wrecked each other's cars. A squealing mother gripped Gavra's arm, but he shook her off, heading down the corridor to the door marked GÜVENLIK. The guard nodded at him, but still refused to smile.

Brano was alone with the fat man. On a table, a reel-to-reel tape player sat inert as both men smoked. Brano said, "Anything on Mas?"

"He cleared out of his hotel room in the Pera Palas, and now he's waiting for a flight back home."

"He's still in the airport?"

"Flight leaves in an hour."

The fat man grunted and said in his heavy accent, "I can not make the sense of it."

"Play it for him," said Brano.

The fat man got up to leave. "You do it. I can not listen more."

Once he was gone, Brano rewound the tape and pressed STOP. Then PLAY.

The voice that came out was staticky, speaking English. ". . . and this is an order, from the Armenian Diaspora across the planet, sufferers of the genocide at the hands of the Turkish imperialists, in solidarity with our freedom-loving comrades in Palestine and West Germany . . ."

"He's reading it," Gavra said.

"Shh."

". . . a hundred thousand in United States dollars and the release from United States prison of the revered Gourgen Mkrtich Yanikian."

Then came another man's voice, clearer: "We understand. Just give us some time. You have enough fuel to remain in the air for—"

"I know this! We know everything. The Armenian nation has—"

The tape squealed as Brano held down the fast-forward button. "A lot of dogma here."

"Who's Gourgen Yanikian?" Gavra asked.

"American citizen, Armenian descent. Two years ago he invited the Turkish consul general and the consul to lunch at the Biltmore Hotel in Santa Barbara, California. He shot them both with a Luger. Killed them."

"Right."

"I suspect," said Brano, "that these people are connected to the Prisoner Gourgen Yanikian Group."

"I remember. Two months ago."

"Yes, in February they committed two acts in Beirut. They tried to bomb the Turkish Information and Tourism Bureau—it went off while police tried to defuse it. Then they set off a bomb in the Turkish Airlines offices."

"I thought the ASALA did that."

Brano shrugged. "The Armenian Secret Army for the Liberation of Armenia also claimed responsibility."

"Too many names," said Gavra.

"Listen to this."

Brano pressed PLAY.

The hijacker was crying now, and through the sobs he spoke Turkish that Brano translated in his monotone. *"She said it. She's one of yours. Yes. Because she knows even more. She told me. How did she know?"*

A click, then the other man said in English, "What did she say to you?"

"Just that . . . that . . ." Brano translated, then stopped because the voice had gone silent.

"Hello?" said the other man. "Are you still there? Come in, five-four."

There was no reply. Brano stared hard at the machine. "That was the last transmission before the explosion. It occurred a couple of minutes later."

" 'She'?"

"I don't know."

Gavra sank into a chair. "A suicide. Then why the demands?"

"That's the question."

"Then let's talk to Mas."

Brano stood up.

The fat Turk's name was Captain Talip Evren, and he found a guard to walk them through the security check. Mas was at Gate 5 with thirty other travelers, reading an old copy of *The Spark,* a leg crossed over his knee.

"Ludvík," said Brano.

Mas looked up, then smiled easily, losing the claustrophobia of before. "Brano. What are you doing in Istanbul?"

"I'd like to ask you the same thing."

"It's the nature of our business we seldom get answers."

"You were always philosophical, Ludvík."

"Who's the kid?"

Gavra said, "Captain Gavra Noukas."

"Noukas?" Mas bit his lip. "I've heard about you."

Brano sat in the chair next to him. "You were waiting for someone. Now you're going back home. That's correct?"

"Well, your boy was following me, so I don't suppose I should lie."

"I want to know what's going on."

Mas folded the newspaper into his lap and spoke with the patient confidence of a much older man. "Brano. Each of us has our orders, and we follow them. Yes, I was waiting for someone, but that someone didn't arrive. I called my contact and learned what happened. It's a tragedy, but the fact is that my job is now over. I'm going home. You'll no doubt be asked to do the same."

"How did your contact learn what happened?"

"My contact keeps his ear to the ground."

A tone sounded, and a uniformed woman at a podium called, "Flight number 603—"

Mas stood. "Let the Turks take care of this. They have an admirable police force." He shook Brano's hand, then Gavra's. His grip was sweaty. "Good to meet you, young man. And stick with Comrade Sev. He's the best there is."

That afternoon, Gavra sat at the Hotel Erboy's small rooftop café, looking over the city while Brano used the telephone at the front desk. His vista included the mouth of the Golden Horn and thick-settled Beyoğlu; in the foreground was a pair of handsome young Germans drinking vodka tonics by the ledge. One noticed him and smiled, then leaned to whisper to his friend, who glanced over and shrugged.

"They want us back home," Brano said as he took the other seat. "There's a flight at eleven in the morning."

"What about the hijacking?"

"Nothing we can do here, and I suspect there won't be much to do in the Capital. The Turks have the passenger manifest, and the Ministry's looking into the records of four Armenians who were on the flight—we should hear something when we return."

"Four Armenians with the exception of Libarid?"

"Yes."

Gavra pulled out a cigarette as a ship in the Bosphorus moaned. "What about Mas? He could be connected to this. Maybe he was also waiting for Libarid."

Brano shook his head. "It's just a terrible coincidence. Libarid was on a plane that some Armenians wanted to use to get back at the Turks. It's bad for us; it's bad for Mas. It's bad for everyone."

"I see."

"And I called the station. Gave the news to Emil. He'll pass it on to Imre and Katja." Brano was squinting in the light.

"Was it hard?"

The old man shrugged. "I've delivered this kind of news often enough. I think it's going to be hard on him, though. Emil Brod does his best, but he's not well equipped to deal with tragedy."

"And you are."

"Well, if I wasn't, I doubt I'd still be alive." Brano paused. "There are only two of us now."

"Two of whom?" Gavra noticed that the Germans were paying their bill and leaving.

"Two veterans." He frowned. "Stefan was killed back in the fifties, and at the same time Ferenc—Ferenc Kolyeszar, you've heard of that samizdat of his, *The Confession*—he was sent into internal exile and has been in a work camp the last three years. And now Libarid." Brano blinked a few times, coming out of his reverie. "You're not going out tonight, are you?"

"What?"

"I don't want to have to kick some poor girl out of your bedroom in the morning," Brano said, but without scorn.

PETER

1968

•

The foreign soldier's beers settled his frayed nerves and helped him drop into a deep, dreamless sleep for hours, until he was woken by gunshots outside. He blinked in the darkness, at first only hearing Josef snoring in the other bed. Peter crawled to the foot of his cot and peered out the window. Down on Pod Stan- icí, against the silhouette of another building, he saw a tiny burst of flame and heard another *rat-a-tat*. He couldn't make out the figure with the gun, nor the intended victim. Boots crunched against the sidewalk, and as he waited for another gunshot he remembered that same sound just outside České Budějovice. A field, a shouted order from the road, then all three of them running westward through the stumps of har- vested corn. Toman ahead of him, Ivana just behind. Toman was cursing—*Fucking Peter, fucking goddamned Peter*—beneath the *rat-a-tat*. Peter looked back in time to catch Ivana's beauti- ful heavy-eyed face suddenly seize up. Then she fell forward, as if she'd tripped. Toman, ahead, was no longer shouting words, only long, painful notes, and Peter realized that he'd passed

Toman's writhing body in the stalks. But he kept on running as the *rat-a-tat* stopped and he heard one of the men at the road shouting at another in Russian. Though he knew Russian, he couldn't make out the words.

"What is it?"

He turned back to see Josef's face emerge from the gloom. "Gunshots. Outside. But I can't see."

Josef rubbed his eyes. "Took days before I could sleep through it." He climbed back into his cot and pulled the sheets to his chin. "Peter?"

"Yeah?"

"How did you get caught? I didn't think there'd be a problem getting across."

Peter looked out at the street. "It was my own fault. I wanted to start a fire."

"A fire?"

"It was cold. We were in a field, and I was cold. Nighttime in the countryside. I hadn't brought a good coat. They told me not to start one, but they were asleep and I was so cold. I didn't think anyone would see."

"But they did."

"The worst luck," said Peter. "A Russian jeep came along the road. And we were woken by the bullhorn. It was morning then. The jeep, it had . . . it had a machine gun on it, and when we ran they fired at us."

"Savages."

He cleared his throat. "We scattered. I can only assume they made it. I went south, and the Russians followed me. They picked me up in the town."

"You were incredibly stupid."

"I know."

"But at least you didn't get anyone killed."

"Yeah," said Peter. He took a breath. "I'm thankful for that."

GAVRA

•

The old man woke him earlier than expected. Six o'clock, and it was just dumb luck, Gavra later reflected, that he had decided to be a good boy the night before. He'd spoken to the Germans in the hotel bar, two Heidelberg cops in town for the Interpol conference. They were attractive and seemed to like Gavra, but after his fifth vodka, he became suspicious of his own judgment. He began hearing the old man's voice in his head. Waking up to Colonel Brano Sev proved he'd been right not to trust himself.

Brano was excited. "The Istanbul police have worked quickly. Last night, they raided an apartment of the Army of the Liberation of Armenia and rounded up three conspirators." He explained this quickly, and Gavra rubbed his eyes, trying to understand.

"One of the men talked," Brano continued. "Turns out they have no connection to the ASALA, the Prisoner Gourgen Yanikian Group, or even the Yanikian Commandos, the ones who tried to set off a bomb in New York two years ago. But guess how they decided to hijack that particular plane, on that day."

"How?"

"A telephone call."

"From who?"

"From Wilhelm Adler."

Only then did Gavra wake fully. Wilhelm Adler, or "Tappi" to the newspapers, had famously spent years in West Germany with the proto-Marxist Red Army Faction, blowing up offices and airport terminals and kidnapping business leaders in an effort to free the older RAF generation—Andreas Baader, Gudrun Ensslin, Horst Mahler, Ulrike Meinhof—from prison. Just as West German police were about to close in on him in June 1974, he crossed into East Germany, and General Secretary Honecker, as always, welcomed the socialist warrior with open arms.

"So East Germany's in on this?"

Brano shook his head. "Adler moved out of Democratic Germany not long after he arrived there. He's been in our country for the last seven months."

"I didn't know."

"Not a lot of people do. Now get your clothes on."

The Turkish *polis* station was not what Gavra expected. Perhaps he expected exotic Muslim arches or policemen sitting on velvet pillows. Instead he found himself in a dirty, gray-walled bureaucratic building not unlike home. In place of a framed portrait of General Secretary Pankov, Kemal Atatürk glared at him from under flaming eyebrows. Then the smell hit him: Turkish tobacco and sweat. It straddled the line between sensual and revolting. At least there was a familiar face: Talip Evren, the fat captain from the airport. He shook their hands with both of his and took them down an empty side corridor. He knocked on a scratched door. The small man who opened it wore a pistol in his belt.

The room was dark, and in the center a young man with hair reaching his shoulders was tied to a chair. A desk lamp shone on his battered face, and the only sound in the room was his labored breathing. Dried blood covered most of his features, so it was hard for Gavra to make out what he looked like.

"May I introduce to you Norair Tigran," said Talip. "Ask as you want and I will make translation."

Brano pulled up a chair and sat just out of the light. "He should tell me everything about Wilhelm Adler."

"Wilhelm?" the young man said, gurgling as if speaking through water. *"Allah belanı versin."*

Talip shook his head. "He does not wish to repeat himself. Hasad."

The small man took out his pistol and swung it into the young man's face.

Gavra thought he heard something snap, but Tigran shifted his head, whispering, "Wilhelm?"

"When did he call?" Brano asked.

Talip translated the answer: *"Last Wednesday."*

"Why was he part of this? He's not Armenian."

"He understand solidarity."

"And he told you to make this a suicide mission?"

Norair Tigran showed his teeth a moment, trying to clear his throat. He spoke, and Talip said: *"It was not suicide mission. He say he don't know what happen."*

"What else did Wilhelm say?"

"*Nothing. Only it must should be that day, that flight. Number five-four.*"

"Why would you listen to him?"

Even through the mask of blood the young Armenian seemed annoyed. He spoke directly to Brano in English. "Because we're new at this, okay? Wilhelm is a veteran. We knew what we wanted to do, but we didn't know when. He told me that this would be the one."

"But why this plane? Why did he say?"

"He said . . ." Norair Tigran cocked his head. "He said it would be the best."

"But *why*?"

"Just that he knew. But Wilhelm—" Norair grunted something like a laugh. "Wilhelm was wrong about this one."

During the interview, Gavra asked no questions. He wanted to, and Brano would have allowed it, but no words came to him. On the flight back home, he said, "It's disappointing. In that room I didn't have the presence of mind to come up with a single question."

Brano told him not to worry. "This case is hardly a case for us. The Turkish police are well equipped to handle the investigation of the hijacking. But since the hijackers boarded in the Capital, we should try to reconstruct what they did in our country and pass that information on to the Turks. We begin with Wilhelm Adler."

Gavra gazed at the seat in front of him. "There's something more here. I'm sure of it."

"Let's talk to Adler," Brano said. "No one will expect extradition to Turkey, but he should be able to shed some light on this."

"Tonight?" Gavra asked as a stewardess collected their empty coffee cups.

"Tomorrow. Our people are keeping an eye on him; he won't get away."

"What about Ludvík Mas?"

Brano scratched his ear. "Ludvík Mas is none of our concern. He works in an office no one looks into, because it's best no one does."

"Do you mean Room 305?"

Brano gave him a blank expression. "That office does not exist." He folded his tray table shut. "And what does not exist should not be thought about."

Brano dropped him off at his Fourth District sixth-floor walk-up a little after four in the afternoon. The pitted field surrounding his apartment block was full of out-of-commission Trabants rusting under the sun. It was Thursday, but even on a workday the familiar trio of young men by the door was sharing a plastic bottle of cheap palinka. A couple of years before, Mujo, the hairi-est of the group, got hold of a smuggled record by an American rock band, the Velvet Underground. His life began sliding down-hill that very day.

"You've been traveling?" said Mujo. "You got some sun."

"Sun and water and lots of sex, Mujo."

The alcoholic told his friends, "Gavra here is a traveler. A man of the *world*." For some reason that made the other two laugh.

"And don't forget," Gavra told them, "I also find volunteers for the state. Someone needs to dig our canals."

The men quieted, unsure whether this was a joke, as Gavra went inside and checked his mailbox, which was empty.

His apartment was small and untidy. The living room was filled with stacks of records: *Leb i Sol*—Bread and Salt, a Yugoslav band he was fond of—some Beatles, as well as an English singer, Elton John. A fine layer of dust covered everything, even the off-green walls. Gavra had become used to the grime over the years; he lived his life outside those walls.

He grabbed a bottle of homemade palinka from the cabinet— a bottle, he remembered as he pulled out the cork, from Libarid's wife's family distillery. He found a fresh pack of cigarettes and settled in front of his little black-and-white television. That's when he saw the story. Earlier in the day, members of the Red Army Faction and the Heidelberg Socialist Patients' Collective took over the West German Embassy in Stockholm. In retaliation for an attempted recovery by Swedish police, they brought the West German military attaché, Baron Andreas von Mirchbach, to a window and put bullets through his head, his leg, and his chest. Police, stripped down to their underwear to show they were un- armed, dragged the body away.

The newscaster, in order to help clarify the groups' aims, quoted Red Army Faction founder Ulrike Meinhof from a state- ment she had made the previous year from Stammheim Prison in Stuttgart:

Faced with the transnational organization of capital, the mili- tary alliances with which U.S. imperialism encompasses the world, the cooperation of the police and secret services, the international organization of the dominant elite within the sphere of power of U.S. imperialism, the response from our side, the side of the prole- tariat, is the struggle of the revolutionary classes, the liberation

*movements of the Third World, and the urban guerrilla in the me-
tropoles of imperialism. That is proletarian internationalism.*

Gavra wondered how anyone, after listening to that, could be
optimistic about international affairs.

KATJA

•

I've been three days with as many hours sleep, but only now do I feel it. Climbing out of the taxi, the hot sun makes me momentarily blind, and the airport is suddenly replaced by a field of dizzying sunspots. When I reach back to the taxi for support, it's already gone, and I stumble into a cloud of hot exhaust.

I'm trying to focus through the fatigue, clutching my small leather purse and counting its contents in my head: a new external passport, some money, and a roll of audiotape.

At the TisAir desk I wait behind a young couple who squeeze each other's hands as they wait for the clerk to stamp their tickets. It seems to take a long time, but I'm not sure. Because time has become strange. Until only a week ago—yes, Wednesday, 23 April—I was faced with the regular minutiae: the sour husband, the paperwork-clogged desk in the militia office, the condescension from my workmates. A frustrating life, being the only woman working homicide, but a simple one to understand.

Now I'm at the counter, explaining to the pert blonde with a blue TisAir cap that I would like to go to Istanbul on the seven o'clock flight.

She scans a list on a clipboard. "Will you be bringing luggage?"

"Just me."

She wields a pen. "And you are?"

"Katja Drdova." I hand over my crisp passport as evidence.

The ticket costs more koronas than I expect, but I count out the money without argument, nodding when she explains that I'll have to also purchase a visa in the Istanbul airport. My skin is beginning to tingle. The exhaustion affects my bones, or it feels that way, as if dirt has wedged its way into my joints. And my senses are becoming acute—an ill woman behind me breathes with the intensity of a tractor engine.

Ticket in hand, I cross the bright tile floor to a small corridor past the pay phones to the bathrooms. I splash water on my face and look in the mirror, prodding the corners of my eyes with a fingertip.

Old.

But I'm only twenty-four.

Given the heavy lids and shallow creases across my brow, it's an understandable mistake.

I consider calling Aron from one of those pay phones. He'll return to an empty house tonight, and, though it won't be so strange, after a while he'll worry. He doesn't deserve that. But what could I tell him? That I'm going to Turkey unexpectedly? That's not something people just do. People just don't do this.

My hands tremble when I show my ticket to the uniformed border guard, but he doesn't seem to notice. At the gate, I ask a fat man with a little red star on his lapel for a cigarette. He smiles glassily as he lights it for me; then I feel him following me with his eyes as I find a seat by the window and smoke, staring at the planes taxiing on the tarmac.

This, I recall, is where Libarid was. Maybe this exact spot.

When the news came a week ago, I was on the telephone with Aron, who had called from the factory to continue our previous night's argument about having children—he's never been able to understand my refusal. Chief Brod opened his office door and leaned against the frame. In my ear, Aron was saying, "I've been patient with you; you know this. You can't say I haven't been patient."

Chief Brod is a simple man who wears his emotions on his sleeve, and when he stood in his doorway with his gray-threaded blond hair parted perfectly, like a schoolboy's, in his face I knew this was something big; it was something tragic.

"Let me call you back," I told Aron.

"This is original, cutting me off in the middle of—"

But I'd hung up, and Imre and I followed Emil into his office.

"It's Libarid," our chief said.

"He's in Istanbul," I said. "Right?"

"Bulgaria."

I grinned—*grinned.* "What's he doing there?"

"Yeah," said Imre. "He got a girlfriend there?"

Emil cleared his throat. "Brano called from Istanbul."

Both Imre and I made faces at that name.

"Libarid's dead," Emil told us, then filled in the details— Armenian terrorists, an explosion—and I found myself repeating *Armenia, Armenians* in my head but making no sense of those words.

Aron and I had dined with Libarid and his family now and then. He was a good man—a poor investigator but a decent person—and an Armenian. His wife, Zara, smiled a lot; she seemed content in a way I used to think was a little stupid. But she served wonderful food, delicious pieces of lamb with yogurt they called *kalajosh* and *lahmajoon,* a lamb-topped pizza. When we left Aron would always mention how contented Libarid seemed with his wife and child. I think he was jealous.

And then Libarid was dead, part of a fireball in the Bulgarian sky.

That was only a week ago. Now I'm joining the other passengers in a crowd around the dark stewardess who does her best to smile as she tries to force everyone into a straight line. It's plainly impossible, so she gives up and takes ticket stubs from whoever offers first and sends us out the door, across the hot tarmac to the plane. The fat man with the red star is a few people ahead, and as we step out under the bright, bewildering sun I watch him put on sunglasses. His head, tilted to the side, eyes covered, looks vaguely mysterious.

That's when I wish I could have brought my gun.

PETER

1968

•

In the morning, Peter and Josef conferred with friends in the empty dormitory canteen. School had been closed indefinitely, but Jan had a key. Peter retold his story humbly—the nighttime fire, the Russian jeep, then running—and they nodded, all confirming his stupidity.

"But why didn't you stick with Toman and Ivana?" asked Gustav, an older, bearded student from the medical school. "Maybe you would've gotten away, too."

"The soldiers were my fault. I'd started the fire. So I had to lead them away from the others."

That earned him a collective nod of respect.

He took a tram into the old town with Jan, and on the way Jan pointed out pockmarked walls—on a cinema, a bakery, a post office. They were in the back of the crowded tram, whispering. "Josef and I were at the radio station, the morning after you left. Radio Prague asked people to come, so we came. Lots of us came." He smiled. "And of course the Russians came, too. It was a terrible fight, took hours. A few times I thought we'd actually make them turn around and leave, but then . . ." He shrugged. "Well, they got through to the station."

"How did you get away?"

"The Russians are stupid. They've got no idea how to work the back streets."

"But they've won."

"Fight's not over yet," Jan said as they got out. He touched his brow. "I'll see you tonight at the meeting."

"What meeting?"

"Didn't Josef tell you? The engineering students are coming, too. Eight o'clock, at the Church of Our Lady of the Snows."

"Right. Of course."

"The priest has a soft spot for us." He winked. "Time to figure out our Plan B."

Peter wandered the town, fists in the pockets of his thin pin-striped jacket, ignoring the forms passing him. He stumbled now and then on concrete broken by the treads of Russian tanks. He had nowhere to be, but at least he wasn't in that old dormitory, surrounded by those students and their proud tales.

What he'd gone through in that field outside České Budějovice, terrible as it had been, was over in a matter of minutes. These students had been plotting and fighting for a week now, and for them it was just the beginning. A sense of valor kept them going. Unlike Jan, Peter had no residual pride to warm himself with.

He considered returning to the Torpédo, just in case that soldier was there to distract him for a while, but in Republic Square he heard a voice.

"Peter Husák."

He turned. In that first second he felt nothing. Then his fingers grew cold and began to fidget in his jacket. Captain Poborsky's bald head glowed in the gray light.

"Now don't tell me you've forgotten me already."

"Of—of course not."

"Can I buy you a coffee?"

"Well, I have to—"

"I insist, Comrade Husák."

The StB officer guided him back to the massive Obecní Dům, the Municipal House. Under the art nouveau glass awning, Peter hesitated, and the captain glanced back with a smile.

"Don't worry, son. You're with me."

That didn't help as they continued into the huge café and followed a maître d' to a small table in the center. Under high chandeliers, Russian commanders in full uniform laughed with Czech apparatchiks and smoked furiously over shots of Becherovka and Smirnoff. This was not a place for students.

The security officer asked the waiter for two cups of café au lait.

"Peter," he said, smiling.

"Yes?"

The officer tugged his mustache. "I've talked to a lot of young men and women over the past weeks, but you—you're interesting."

"I'm not."

"Don't be modest. My world—an interrogator's world—is a world of secrets. My visitors protect those secrets with lies. The lies are usually simple enough—*I didn't do this, or that*—but you . . ." He wagged a finger. "Your lie puzzles me. You say you watched your friends cross into Austria, yes?"

Peter nodded as the waiter set down their cups and backed away.

"See? This is my confusion. The lie can only serve to incriminate you, as an accomplice to criminal human smuggling. When the fact—as today's list of casualties proves—is that Toman Samulka and Ivana Vogler were shot down in a cornfield the day before you were picked up."

Peter looked at his dirty fingernails. "I guess they came back."

"That's reasonable, right?" The captain paused. "No, I'm afraid it's not. Because the report also states there was a third person in that field. A man who escaped because the gun on the jeep jammed." He bobbed his eyebrows. "Pretty lucky man, you are."

Peter took a sip of his coffee—hot milk singed his tongue. "I don't know who that was."

"Who?"

"The man who got away."

The officer wagged his finger again. "Look at you! You've got the talent. You can keep a straight face—you don't even blush!"

"I don't know what you're talking about."

"What I'm talking about, Comrade Husák, is that you have a talent that shouldn't go to waste. It's not important to me what happened down at the border, but whatever happened, you'd rather lie to me than let it be known."

Peter blinked because the cigarette smoke and crystal-refracted light were drying his eyes. "Nothing happened at the border."

"You really are good," said Poborsky. "I've looked at your record. Up until two months ago, you were a fine student. You studied your . . . music? You avoided marches. You didn't even take part in socialist rallies."

"Politics aren't my concern."

"Good, good. Because, between you and me, I hate zealots, no matter what side they're on. They shout so much it hurts my poor ears." He smiled. "You know, I'm told all the time that everything is political. Man, our socialist teachers explain, is a political animal, and, in fact, the personal *is* the political. But between you and me, I've never believed that. The political, in fact, is really only the personal dressed up in more flamboyant clothes. There is no political man, only men, whose politics grow from their personal traumas. You follow me?"

Peter didn't answer, but Poborsky nodded as if he had. "I see you do."

Peter knew where all this was leading, but he wanted the captain to spell it out. "Why are you telling me this?"

"Because I think your route in life is still to be charted. Because I think you are made for better things than musicology."

Peter finished his coffee and set down the empty cup. The officer took a slip of paper from his pocket and placed it on the table. There was a phone number written on it.

"Take it," he said.

Peter folded the paper into his jacket pocket. "Can I go now?"

"Who's keeping you?" Comrade Poborsky leaned forward and whispered, "There's another world out there. Just call that number when you're ready."

"For recruitment?"

"Recruitment or information. Whatever you feel is within your power."

Peter walked out of the Obecní Dům.

GAVRA

•

The metro brought him to the First District militia station, to homicide. Unlike many buildings that had been torn down and reconstructed in the socialist mold, this station retained its form from before the war. Habsburg flourishes decorated the high, narrow window frames and, along the third floor, cracked maidens gazed protectively down at the street. The cracks continued inside, twisting along the buckling walls, painted over every few months in pale green.

Brano Sev had kept a desk there, on and off, for the past thirty years. As his apprentice, Gavra shared it. At the three other desks sat Katja and Imre, whom he greeted. The third desk was banally empty, and for an instant Gavra wondered if he'd be given Libarid's desk. He was tired of pulling up a spare chair beside Brano.

The thought made him want to hit himself.

Katja and Imre—his feet propped on his desk as he spoke on the telephone—nodded back at him but didn't say a word. There was a palpable gloom over the office. Brano didn't look up at him, but that wasn't unusual, because the old man came into this business at the end of the war, when state security agents learned how to let people hate them. He created distance with everyone, because he believed that it served him better this way.

Katja had never made a secret of hating Brano, and Imre, in his quiet way, felt the same. Even Chief Emil Brod, despite the obligations of his job and their long shared history, was never warm with Brano Sev, as he was with the rest of them. Brano Sev was a peculiar man.

Gavra paused at Katja's desk. "How's it coming so far?"

She tugged some blond hair behind her ear as her phone began to ring. "I'm going to check with the Hotel Metropol today. We only just got the names from the passenger manifest."

She sounded tense, and she was squeezing a pen tightly. The phone continued to ring. "You going to answer that?"

She looked at the phone, then shook her head. "I know who it is."

"What's wrong?" he asked in a lowered voice.

"Nothing. Look, I wanted you to come along to the hotel, but the *Com*rade says you're going to be occupied."

"Take Imre," he whispered.

Katja rolled her eyes. It was common knowledge that Imre Papp was a dunce. "Why can't you come?"

"We're interviewing a suspect."

"Gavra," said Brano, using a finger to call him over.

"What suspect?" asked Katja.

Imre, by the window, covered the telephone mouthpiece with his palm. "We've got a suspect?"

"It's not for public discussion," said Brano. "Gavra. Over here."

As he moved to the old man's desk, Katja said, "This is typical. Just the kind of lackluster help I've come to expect."

Gavra pulled up a chair, and Brano leaned close. "I pointed out yesterday that it's not common knowledge Wilhelm Adler is in this country. Let's try to keep it that way."

Just then the far door, marked CHIEF, opened, and Emil Brod stepped out. The small, graying man always had an air of confusion about him, and when he saw Gavra he looked for an instant as if he couldn't remember who he was. "Gavra," he said finally, coming forward and offering a hand. "Any news?"

"I only know what Brano's told me."

"Okay," said Emil, rubbing fingers through his hair. "Keep me posted."

The chief returned to his office as Brano grabbed his hat. "Come on, Gavra."

In the car, Brano handed him a slip of paper with four names. "The hijackers arrived in the Capital on the twentieth, last Sunday, from Istanbul."

Gavra read:

> Emin Kazanjian
> Sahag Manoogian
> Jirair Keshishian
> Zareh Petrossian

"They stayed two nights in the Hotel Metropol and then boarded Flight 54. They made no phone calls, and they had no visitors. As far as the Ministry can tell, they never left the hotel."

"Why didn't you tell Katja? She's going to waste a day finding this same information."

Brano paused, then said, "I don't want that girl getting in the way."

Gavra looked again at the paper. Two nights in the Metropol, no visitors, then direct to the airport. "How did they get the explosives?"

"It's not hard," said Brano as they passed an old woman selling homemade brooms. "Someone could visit the hotel restaurant at the same time as them and leave a package. If it was all arranged from Istanbul, there's no way for us to track it down. But if Adler was involved . . ."

"Libarid would have had access to explosives," said Gavra.

Brano chose not to answer.

After a grand escape from the Federal Republic of Germany in mid-1974, Wilhelm Adler spent three months in the German Democratic Republic, handing the Stasi all the information he had on the Red Army Faction's present hierarchy and the security measures of the West German industrial elite. In return, they gave him an East German passport. He worked briefly at the Hotel Unter den Linden in East Berlin before meeting and falling in love with Buba Polinski, a tourist who, once the paperwork was settled, brought him back to the Capital with her. Since then he'd held a job at the Sachet Automotive Works, on the edge of the Tenth District, piecing together carburetors and sending them down the line.

When the supervisor pointed him out through the window of his office, they saw a slumped back, a small man, thin. Gavra was surprised by this. He'd read of Adler's exploits with his RAF brethren: the bank robberies where they wore rubber Willy Brandt masks and distributed some of their withdrawals to the kidnapped customers; and the low-level politicians they photographed in captivity, then threw from fast-moving cars once they'd received their ransom. Gavra expected someone more erect.

The factory stank of grease, and the noise of the machinery was deafening, so Brano only tapped Adler on the shoulder. The German was neither unnerved nor taken aback by the sight of Brano's Ministry card, nor did he hesitate when Brano nodded at the metal stairs leading up to the supervisor's office. He followed Brano while Gavra walked behind them. Once inside, Brano said to the supervisor, "A moment alone, please?"

The supervisor, a big man, reddened and rushed out.

Adler sat at the desk. "What is it this time?"

"A couple of questions." Brano sat across from him. Gavra remained standing, hands crossed over his groin, like a heavy in an American noir film.

Brano placed his hat in his lap. "Are you familiar with the Army of the Liberation of Armenia?"

Adler shrugged. "I've heard some things. I'm still in touch with my friends on the other side. My old comrades are putting up a good stand in Stockholm."

"That's already over," said Brano.

Adler knotted his brows but didn't speak.

Gavra said, "Last week, you made an international call to Norair Tigran in Istanbul. You told him about a particular Turkish Airlines flight, number 54, leaving from here, bound for there. You suggested he hijack it."

Adler rooted in his ear with a finger. "Did he hijack it?"

"His colleagues hijacked it."

"I hadn't heard."

"Because it hasn't yet made our papers. Tonight's edition."

"I see."

"Tigran is in prison."

"That's too bad."

Gavra, despite himself, was impressed by this small, slumped man. He spoke as if the conversation were about lost dogs. Of course, Wilhelm Adler had been through a lot, and compared with the rest of his life, this interview was nothing.

"What about the four men?" Gavra asked.

He looked at Gavra. "What four men?"

"The ones who did the job. When did you give them the explosives?"

"I don't know what you're talking about."

Gavra looked at Brano, and Brano nodded. So Gavra squatted beside the chair. He smiled up at Adler. "Have you ever been interrogated before?"

Adler grinned. "Of course. The BND put me through it at Stammheim."

He patted the German's knee. "No. I mean an interrogation."

Adler crossed his hands over his stomach. "That's what I just said."

Brano walked to the windows overlooking the factory and lowered the blinds.

Adler said, "I'm not a little boy, comrades. I fought for the workers' state."

"Did you?" said Brano.

"I've killed five leaders of imperial capitalism. Two politicians, a bank owner, a—"

He stopped because Gavra had punched the side of his head. He gritted his teeth, blinking.

Gavra's knuckles tingled as he spoke. "I don't care what you've done, comrade. I only care what you tell me now. Inside this little office anything can happen. To me, there's no one in this whole factory except the three of us."

"But I don't know anything!"

Brano watched as Gavra clutched the German's hair and threw his head on the desk. It bounced. Gavra squatted again. "Listen, comrade. Sixty-eight people are dead, and one of them was a colleague of mine. I was fond of him. You're the one who dictated what flight would be blown up, and you're the only one I have my hands on."

"Blown up?" he said, confused. "They weren't supposed to blow it up." He wasn't able to see very well.

"What were they supposed to do?" asked Brano.

"Money—just money. And to free some comrades."

"How did you know Norair Tigran?"

"A few years ago. West Berlin. A Marxist discussion group."

"Okay, then," said Brano. "Why that plane? Why that day?"

"A phone call."

Brano straightened.

"What phone call?" said Gavra.

"I get them sometimes, all right? My old comrades know where to find me. But this was from a local. I suppose it was one of your guys."

"Our guys?"

"From the Ministry."

Gavra hesitated. "What did this person say?"

He sniffed. "Just to call Norair. Tell him about the plane. That plane, that day. He knew they were trying to decide when to pull it off."

"Did he say who he was?" asked Brano.

"Of course not."

"So why," said Brano, "did you listen to him?"

Adler seemed briefly confused; then a trace of contempt entered his voice. "Are you guys for real?"

Gavra put a fist into his stomach, doubling the German over. "Answer the question."

Adler took a few breaths. "These kinds of calls, I don't question them. Yalta Boulevard has its own agenda, doesn't it? We help liberation movements all over the world."

Gavra wasn't sure what to believe. He leaned over the German. "These men. They arrived in town on Sunday. And you met them at the Metropol to give them the explosives. Didn't you?"

"No," he said.

Gavra grabbed his ears. He tried to pull away, but by then Gavra had put his knee into his face. His nose started to bleed, and his eyes were dripping as Gavra squatted again. "Tell me the truth."

"But I am," he whispered, then wiped his nose and examined the blood on his fingers. "I wasn't even here. I was in Sárospatak, in a hotel on the Bodrog River. With my wife. We came back late Tuesday. *Ask her.*" He coughed. "I swear I didn't speak to anyone again after my phone call."

Brano shrugged and said, "Of course you were in the country-side. We have your hotel registration."

Gavra looked up. "What?"

"Come on," said Brano. Then, to Adler: "Remember, you're being watched."

PETER

1968

•

In the tram, looking over the tired faces of his people, Peter knew that Captain Poborsky was right—he had lied about what had happened in that field, and lying was something he was adept at. He'd learned it at home, with his father. But he hadn't lied when he said he would never leave Czechoslovakia.

He had followed his friends to the border out of a need to be with Ivana and knew that once they reached the border he would stop. Or he would cross but, after a few weeks or months, turn around again. He had grown up in this country, had known it all his life, and in this system he had studied music and built his modest world. To Peter, each system was as uncomfortable as the next; it only mattered which one you had become accustomed to.

He was back at the dormitory in a half hour. The corridor was as smoky as the café had been, with faces he recognized lining the walls. A few nodded, but most ignored him. They were part of a steady undertone of conversation that, before the Russians arrived, had been an overtone. At least that was something positive about the Russians' appearance: It was quieter now.

When he opened the door to 305, a hand grabbed his shirt, pulled and threw him heavily on his cot. His head knocked against the wall. Josef stood over him, his dark features flushed. Behind Josef, Gustav from the medical school reclined on the other cot, watching calmly and scratching his beard.

"What the hell's going on?" said Peter, sitting up.

Josef slammed the door shut. "Where were you, Peter?"

"I was in town, with Jan."

"After that."

"I came here."

Josef stepped closer—he was very quick—and punched the side of Peter's head. Ringing erupted in his ear.

Gustav, from the cot, said, "Don't lie to us. We know you met an StB agent in the Obecní Dům."

"The fucking Obecní Dům!" said Josef.

Gustav said, "Jan saw you."

"Was I being followed?"

"I could kill you," said Josef.

"What did you tell him?" asked Gustav.

"I didn't tell him anything."

Josef hit the side of his head again.

Peter raised a hand. "Cut that out, okay? I'm telling you I didn't say a thing. I don't *know* anything."

"What did he want?" asked Gustav.

Peter flinched when Josef moved closer. "He wanted to scare me. He wanted names, of course. But I'm telling you, I didn't give him any."

"You were with him for a while," said Josef.

"Well, you don't just stand up and walk out when you're dealing with these men. Do you?"

"I'd have strangled him."

"No you wouldn't have," said Gustav. He rubbed his bloodshot eyes, scratched his beard again, then looked up when someone knocked at the door. "Yeah?"

Jan poked his head in. "Josef, can we—" He noticed Peter on the cot. "Josef, can I talk to you out here?"

Josef closed the door as he left, and Peter looked at Gustav. "You don't think I betrayed anyone, do you?"

"I don't know what to think." He stifled a yawn. "But you can appreciate that we've got to be careful."

"Of course."

"Josef likes to jump to conclusions."

"He's never trusted me."

Gustav lit a cigarette and offered one. Peter took a drag, closing his eyes. "So what's on the agenda?"

"What agenda?"

"My agenda?"

"You'll be ostracized, at least until we can assure ourselves you're not . . . one of them."

Peter crossed a leg over his knee. "At least I'll have time to study."

"What if the policeman comes back?"

"I can't tell him what I don't know."

Josef returned, his face a deeper red than before. He moved slowly as he sat beside Gustav.

"Well?" said Gustav.

Josef blinked. "It seems Peter hasn't been completely honest."

"Oh?" said Gustav.

"Oh?" echoed Peter.

Josef spoke through his teeth. "Today's list of casualties went up an hour ago. Guess what?"

"What?" asked Peter.

"Go ahead. Guess."

"Don't screw around," said Gustav. "Tell us."

"No," said Josef. "I want this bastard to take a stab in the dark."

Peter shrugged, because though he knew, it was best not to know, and so he cleared the knowledge from his head.

"Come on," said Gustav.

Josef leaned forward and patted Peter's cheek with an open hand, then gripped his ear. "Ivana and Toman are on the list. They were killed outside České Budějovice."

"That's horrible," said Peter. He tried to pull his ear out of Josef's grip but couldn't.

"Remember his story?" said Josef. "He bravely led the Russians away from his friends, who he'd gotten into a tough spot." He twisted Peter's ear just a little, so it hurt. "They didn't make it out of that field, did they?"

"I don't know," Peter began, then grunted. "I don't know what you're talking about."

"He killed them," said Josef. "His stupidity killed them, and he won't even admit it."

Gustav straightened. "That's what it sounds like."

"They were alive," said Peter. "I last saw them alive."

Josef punched him in the eye. He fell back, his head hitting the wall again.

Gustav leaned his elbows on his knees. "What are we going to do with you?"

"We can't believe anything he says," said Josef.

"No. We can't." Gustav stood up. "Come on. We'll talk to the others and take a vote." Peter began to stand, but Gustav held up a finger. "Not you. You stay here. The door will be watched. You understand?"

Peter nodded.

GAVRA

•

Gavra was furious. He had brutalized a man who, though not innocent in the classical sense, was not guilty of the particular thing Gavra was thinking of as he put his knee into his face.

"Why did you do that?"

Brano turned onto Mihai Boulevard and cocked his head. "I wanted you to keep the pressure on. If you believed Adler had given them the explosives, then you'd push him. He didn't move the explosives himself, but if he knew who had done it he would have said something. He didn't know."

Gavra watched the gray Tisa flowing past. Everyone in the Militia office hated Brano Sev, and he was beginning to understand exactly why. Brano understood people; he knew them well enough to know what to say, or do, to most trouble them. And for Gavra, this method was finally showing results.

When he was ten, Gavra's father told him that a wild dog lived just outside their village, and that it ate children. When he realized that this was a lie to keep him from wandering, Gavra began to hate his father. Two decades later, his Ministry mentor was doing the same thing.

Gavra lit a cigarette. "We need to look at the Ministry. Someone at Yalta called Wilhelm Adler and told him what information to pass on."

"We don't know it was someone from the Ministry," said Brano. "Adler doesn't know—he's just guessing."

"Ludvík Mas was waiting at the airport. He's involved."

"We were at the airport," Brano countered. "Does that mean we're involved?"

Gavra cracked the window to let out smoke. "You know what most bothers me?"

"Tell me."

"You're choosing to ignore the biggest connection—or coincidence. Whatever you want to call it."

"Then enlighten me, Gavra."

"Why was Libarid, the only Armenian in the Militia, on a plane taken over by Armenian terrorists?"

Brano didn't answer at first. He turned onto Karl Liebknecht, a small side street filled with vegetable shops, and parked. "Continue."

"I just think it shouldn't be overlooked."

"Do you propose speaking to Zara, his widow? One day after she's learned her husband was killed?"

Brano was testing him; he knew that. The old man always looked him in the eyes when he wanted to measure Gavra's abilities. "Why not?"

"Okay," Brano said as he started the car again. "Let's go see her."

They parked in a narrow, muddy lot in the Tenth District, between block towers riddled with terraces hemmed in by opaque colored glass. Each piece of glass was cracked. They took a loud elevator to the fifth floor and found TERZIAN on a plaque beneath an eyehole. "Go ahead," said Brano.

Gavra pressed the buzzer.

From inside came a woman's voice, "Vahe . . . Vahe, no!" Then footsteps, and a pause as she peered through the eyehole. Zara opened the door, a robe pulled tight around her small body, her face swollen, her eyes slits. "Brano. Gavra."

"How are you?" said Gavra.

She looked at him as if the question made no sense. She glanced back. "Come in."

They sat in the cramped living room, trying not to step on Vahe's wooden toys, which were scattered across the carpet, though the boy was nowhere to be seen.

"Can I get you some coffee?"

"No, thank you, Zara," said Gavra.

Brano shook his head; he was choosing silence.

She sat in a stiff wooden chair and put her hands together between her knees, as if in prayer. "Did you catch them?"

"We're working on it," said Gavra.

She nodded, and Gavra noticed Brano was suddenly distracted, looking at the wall. To the left of the television hung a large cross decorated at the ends with ornate swirls.

"Which is why we're here," Gavra continued. "These terrorists, the ones who were responsible. I guess you know they were Armenian."

She nodded again.

"So we're trying to follow up on any possible connection." He cleared his throat as she stared at him. He should have thought this through before coming here. "During the past few weeks, did you or Libarid have any contact with Armenians you didn't previously know?"

"You're asking if we've been talking to terrorists?"

He shook his head. "No. What I mean is, the Armenian community here is very small, and it makes sense that if new people arrived, it would be well known."

She sighed. "Gavra, when people leave the Armenian Soviet Socialist Republic, they don't come here. They go to Moscow, or Belgrade, or even New York. But not here. The Armenians you find in our country had the bad fortune of being born here."

She bit her lip, as if what she'd said hadn't come out right. From a back room, Gavra heard the child humming.

"Do you go to church?" Brano asked, nodding at the cross.

Zara's cheekbones reddened, and she smiled at him, but it wasn't a kind smile. Her small eyes were pink. "Comrade Sev, my husband may have kept our religion a secret, but I'm not my husband. Here." She reached back to the bookcase behind her and grabbed a thick book called *Orations*—the collected writings of General Secretary Tomiak Pankov. She opened it to show that the guts had been ripped out and replaced with a leather-bound book, gold squiggly letters across the cover. "Here it is, comrade. I'm not going to hide my Bible anymore. Want to read?"

Brano said nothing, only leaned back and crossed his arms over his stomach, while Gavra tilted forward, elbows on his knees.

"We're not here to make accusations, Zara. We're trying to figure out what happened to Libarid."

Zara closed the book as Vahe stumbled into the room, grinning. There was a smudge of dirt across his forehead. When he saw the men, he stopped. "Come here," Zara said, and he approached warily. She replaced the book in her lap with her son, wet her thumb with her tongue, and wiped his forehead clean.

"Hey, buddy," said Gavra, smiling, but the boy didn't answer.

"Comrade Terzian," said Brano, "I asked my question because the church, as the center of the Armenian community, may have some answers for us."

She nodded, then squeezed her son to her breast. "Sorry. I—I've lost the only thing I could depend on. Libarid was the one person in my life devoted completely to me—to *us*—and now I'm left with only a memory. I . . ." She kissed the crown of Vahe's head; he rolled his eyes. "This is no fake emotion, you see. It's real. It makes rational thought a little difficult. No—we didn't hear about any new Armenians. We knew about Gourgen Yanikian, of course, like everybody, but that's America for you. America encourages people to do things like shoot each other." She paused. "But I don't know anyone who approved of Yanikian's killings."

Then she started to cry, but her son smiled at them, as if to say, *Look at her, would you?*

At the Militia station, Katja was standing by the window, alone. She looked up as they entered and said, "Any leads?"

"No," Brano said before Gavra could open his mouth. "And you? Any luck at the hotel?"

She wagged a finger at him. "The desk clerk told me you'd already been there. Would you call that a lead?"

"Perhaps," said Brano, then went to his desk and began to dial the phone.

Once Brano was looking in the other direction, Katja raised her eyebrows at Gavra and pointed at the door, before walking out through it.

The old man was hunched over the mouthpiece, talking quietly to someone as Gavra followed her out.

He found her on the front steps, smoking a cigarette. "What's going on?"

"Come on," she said. "Let's get a drink."

She led him to the underground parking lot and took a Militia Škoda. She drove them to a smoky café-bar on October Square. On the way, she only said, "I'm not going to talk to the old bastard. Only to you. Because I know you'll work with me on this. Am I right?"

"Yes," said Gavra, unsure. "Of course."

They said hello to Max and Corina—the couple gave discounts to the Militia, which made their café popular with the station—and ordered palinkas. Gavra waited for the drinks, then carried them to the window table where Katja sat.

She smiled—Katja often smiled at Gavra, and he worried that she was flirting with him. He knew she had difficulties in her marriage, and in Gavra's experience marital troubles raised the chances he'd find himself in the embarrassing situation of fending off a female advance. Women sensed something in him that, unlike their men at home, was unthreatening.

She hadn't invited him out for anything like that, though. "Brano thought he trumped me by letting me go to the hotel when he'd already been. But the old comrade doesn't quite know everything."

Gavra leaned closer.

"He asked the staff if the Armenians had talked to anyone while they were there—phone calls, meetings in their rooms—and they hadn't. But I found a very cooperative desk clerk who

seemed to like me. I had him go through their records again, and
he came up with this."

She produced a slip of paper marked

Hotel Metropol

MESSAGE

TIME: 23:44

TO: *Emin Kazanjian*
FROM: *Cd. Martrich*

Gavra took it. "No message, no first name?" He turned the paper to look at its blank reverse. "Just *Comrade Martrich*?"

She shrugged.

"Why didn't they give this to Brano?"

"Because," she said, "the message never reached the hijackers.
Comrade Martrich called *after* they had checked out and left for
the airport. Look at the time."

"About an hour before—"

"—the plane took off," she said. "But that's nothing. I thought
the name was familiar, so I went back to Flight 54's passenger
manifest. Tenth line down, Zrinka Martrich."

"A woman? On the same flight?"

Katja looked very pleased with herself. "So I sent Imre to Victory Square to look up her file. Almost nothing there at all. But
just try to guess her last known address."

"What?"

"Guess!" She was enjoying this.

"I don't know," said Gavra.

Katja placed her hands flat on the table. "A mental asylum, just outside Vuzlove. The Tarabon Residential Clinic."

Gavra opened his mouth but was too stunned to speak.

She said, "I'm thinking this woman was insane."

"An insane accomplice to hijacking?"

Katja shrugged. "Now you."

"Me?"

"Yes. Tell me what you and the *Com*rade have learned."

Which is what he did.

KATJA

•

The stewardess smiled when I asked for water, but that was twenty minutes ago, and now she's talking to the fat man in first class. He flicks his little red star self-consciously, flirting, and the stewardess is so flattered she's forgotten my drink.

There's a middle-aged man snoring beside me. Before passing out he tried to start a conversation, informing me that he was to meet with some extremely important Turks to discuss exporting locally made electric fans. "We're famous for manufacturing the best fans in the region, did you know that? Better even than the Poles, and they're admirable competition."

"Interesting," I told him, then turned away and asked for water.

His face is now pressed into the cushion of the headrest, his mouth flaccid and damp.

Up front, the stewardess laughs liltingly.

So I wave until she notices, touches the fat man's sleeve to ask his patience, and walks over.

"Yes?" The stewardess squats beside me, showing off her intense brown eyes.

"That water, please."

"Water?"

"Yes. I asked for water a while ago."

"I see," she says, though it's plain she doesn't. "I was just getting that."

Or maybe, I think as the stewardess continues to the rear of the plane, it's just that unreliable sense of time. Maybe I did only just ask for the water, and the stewardess has decided I'm one of the troublesome passengers, one of the bitches.

As if to confirm this, the fat man grunts and twists in his seat so he can get a good look at me.

I find myself wishing the fan salesman awake. Conversation would at least distract me from the fact that I'm having trouble remembering the last week. There are details—the explosion of the Turkish Airlines flight. The insane asylum. And the trail leading to a dead woman and her brother, Adrian. Adrian Martrich. And, of course, Gavra.

Out of the week there are only three vivid faces that remain with me, all men. Gavra, Adrian, and *him*. But I've lost track of what connects them all. Why were we protecting Adrian Martrich? Gavra never would explain anything in detail. Soon after the investigation started he became cold and uncommunicative.

And then, two days ago, Adrian Martrich suggested we go out for a drive. "Where?"

He shrugged. "To someplace I think you'll be interested in."

A voice is speaking to me.

It's the stewardess, holding a plastic cup. "You did want water, right?"

"Of course. Thank you."

The stewardess hands it over, smiles briefly, and returns to the fat man, shaking her head as she speaks to him.

I drink the whole cup in one go and crush it into the pocket of the next seat.

There is a part of me that tries not to remember that short trip with Adrian Martrich, because when I recall its details I shake and the surety of what I'm doing begins to collapse. So I jump to Wednesday morning—*this* morning—when I called the Militia station. Imre, that poor dunce, had spent the last week completely in the dark; I treated him with the same silence Gavra gave me, and when I called I was in no mood to fill him in. "Get me Brano Sev."

"Brano?" said Imre.

"Just get him, will you?"

Imre timidly called for our Ministry officer to please take the phone.

"Sev here."

"This is Katja."

"Good morning, Katja."

"Where's Gavra?"

"I don't know. I haven't heard from him."

"Can we meet?"

"You don't want to speak in the office?"

"No."

He sighed. "Can you make it to the Hotel Metropol at noon?" He sounded so much more accommodating than he naturally was. "The bar."

GAVRA

•

Saturday morning Gavra cleaned himself and put on his dress uniform. He'd never felt comfortable in it, because, as he left Unit 16, his neighbors, including Mujo and his closest friend, Haso (already drunk, though it was only nine o'clock), paused to watch him pass.

He met the others at the Seventh District cemetery, where the tight crabgrass clung to the earth, and waited as Chief Brod said a few clumsy words in front of the hole, then stepped back to let two young recruits shoot rifles into the air. There was nothing left of Libarid Terzian to bury; inside the cheap coffin lay Libarid's best suit, cleaned and pressed by Zara the day before.

Gavra shook little Vahe's hand as if he were now a man, then turned to Zara, who looked away as he spoke.

"My condolences, Zara. And I'm sorry if yesterday—"

"Don't," she said, then rubbed her arm.

So he withdrew past Katja and Imre, to where Brano stood on the edge of the crowd in civilian clothes. He held a newspaper under his arm and wore his hat, which struck Gavra as impolite. "Were you close to him?" he asked Brano.

When the old man spoke, his lips didn't move. "We worked in the same office for three decades. We knew each other. I'm not sure you could say we were close."

Gavra surveyed the mourners. There were a lot of people he didn't know, Libarid's friends from outside the station. Armenians mostly, like his wife's family, remnants of various exoduses from greater Turkey in the early part of the century. They didn't look like terrorists. He said, "Katja and I are going to Vuzlove after this."

Brano squinted. "Why?"

"A woman from Flight 54 called and left a message for the hijackers at the hotel."

"Who told you this?"

"Katja uncovered it. The call was made not long before the flight took off, and if the woman knew the hijackers, she had to know they weren't in the hotel—they were with her, in the airport. Interesting, no?" When Brano didn't answer, he added, "Her last address was a mental asylum in Vuzlove."

Brano blinked a few times. "Mental asylum?"

"I'll let you know if anything turns up."

"Name?"

"Eh?"

"This woman's name."

"Martrich," said Gavra. "Zrinka Martrich."

Brano ran his tongue behind his lips, then nodded.

"You know her?"

"No," he said. "I don't want you to waste too much time on this. It's disturbing that someone we knew was a victim of this tragedy, but in the end it's exactly what it looks like: a hijacking that went wrong."

"I'd still like to know why the plane exploded."

"People make mistakes all the time, Gavra. Even terrorists."

Brano handed him the morning's *Spark*. The front page told him that, during their interrogation of Wilhelm Adler, Brano had been right about Stockholm. Though Adler's revolutionary comrades once again showed their frustration by shooting Doctor Heinz Hillegart, the West German economic attaché, no concessions were made by the Swedish authorities. Then, at midnight, the TNT they'd piled in the embassy basement exploded, killing Ulrich Wessel of the Red Army Faction. Everyone else, hostages included, survived. The cause of the explosion was cited as "bad wiring."

"Mistakes are made every day," said Brano, just before he walked across the grass to his car.

Katja drove at top speed along the dusty roads east of the Capital, and Gavra asked why her husband, Aron, hadn't shown up at the funeral—he did, after all, know Libarid. She admitted that they'd been fighting. "He's a good man, though."

"You wouldn't have married him otherwise."

"I might have. Maybe I wouldn't have if I'd known how weak he was. He's desperate for me to find a safe job and have a baby."

"And that's not what you want?"

"What about you? Why aren't you married?"

"No time," he said quickly. Then: "I'm not sure I'd want to bring someone into this kind of life."

She tapped the wheel. "You're different, though. You're not like those other Ministry characters. You don't try to intimidate everyone like Brano does. I don't know how you can work with that man."

"He's my mentor—I see a side of him no one else sees."

"I'd rather not see him at all."

Gavra let the silence sit between them, and he knew why: A small part of him was trying intimidation. Stay silent, and let her project her fears onto you. He only spoke when they saw the sign for Vuzlove on the side of the road. "We're here."

An old man with a white beard gave them directions to the clinic on the north side of town, and they parked beside a lone concrete box in the middle of a grassy field, surrounded by a high barbed-wire fence—the Tarabon Residential Clinic.

"Listen, Gavra," Katja said as she removed the ignition key. "If I insulted you back there—"

"It's nothing." He waved a hand casually, but as he climbed out a smile crept into his face. He was finally getting the hang of it.

The front office was a depressing affair, with two white-smocked matrons in front of a wall of file cabinets, filling ash-trays and watching a black-and-white television in the corner. It was half past three on a Saturday, and like most of the country they were tuned to *Family Popa,* about the difficult but virtuous lives of the members of that ideal socialist family. Gavra had watched it only once and had been irritated by its forced interna-tionalism. While the family's ethnicity was Romanian, they went out of their way to name the children Laszlo (Hungarian), Fran-tisek (Czech), Nastasiya (Ukrainian), and Elwira (Polish).

Katja waved her Militia documents, but neither woman stood as she explained what she needed.

"Eh?" said the closest one.

Gavra took out his Ministry certificate, hoping that would help. It did.

It was intimidating.

The head nurse stood with some effort, finally noticing their dress uniforms. "I'm sorry, I didn't hear what you asked for."

Gavra said, "We're interested in the records of a patient with the family name of Martrich."

She put out her cigarette. "First name?"

"Zrinka."

The nurse went to the wall of drawers and opened *M–P,* then returned with two files: MARTRICH P and MARTRICH S. But the two names were PAUL and SANDOR.

"Zrinka," said Katja. "We're looking for a female patient."

"Well, these aren't women," said the nurse.

"I know."

"And they're the only Martriches here."

Gavra leaned on the counter. "Could she be filed somewhere else?"

"If it's not here—"

"Zrinka?" said the other nurse, her eyes still on the television. "She's been gone three years."

"Where's her file?" said Katja.

"Arendt," said the one at the television.

"Arendt?" Gavra asked.

The first nurse shrugged. "Doctor Arendt. You think so, Klara?"

"He was Zrinka's doctor," said Klara.

"Can we speak to the doctor?" Gavra asked.

"Not here you can't," Klara said to the television.

The other nodded. "He's in the Capital. Left how many?"

"Eight."

"That's right. Eight months ago. Took his patients' files with him."

"You find the doctor," said Klara, "and you'll find your file."

"And where," Gavra said, "do we find the doctor?"

The first nurse hesitated. "Well . . ."

Klara didn't take her eyes off the screen. "Bottom drawer, next to the thumbtacks."

Doctor Arendt lived in an airy third-floor Habsburg apartment over a post office, facing a cobbled Fifth District street. When he opened the door, he froze for an instant in the face of the two uniforms.

"What can I do for you?"

Katja gave him a reassuring smile. "Just a few questions, Comrade Doctor. About an old patient of yours. May we come in?"

Arendt recovered from his surprise and ushered them in. Once they reached the living room, he offered tea, which Katja accepted but Gavra didn't; he was still working on the subtleties of intimidation.

Arendt was an old man, and when he brought Katja's tea, some spilled into the saucer. He settled in his musty purple armchair and put on a smile. Gavra couldn't decide whether it was true or not—this man was a psychologist, so it could have meant anything.

Katja sipped her tea, then said, "We'd like to see the file on a patient of yours. Zrinka Martrich."

Arendt shrugged. "I haven't seen her in three years."

"Still," said Gavra, "we'd like to see the file."

Arendt climbed out of his chair again and went to a wardrobe standing by the bedroom door. Inside were rows of out-of-date files. Zrinka Martrich's folder was thick, covering the seven years, Arendt explained, that she was kept at the Tarabon Residential Clinic. Gavra began to leaf through the heady mix of typed and handwritten memos, cardiograms, dietary records, and interview transcripts but closed it again. "Can you just tell us about her?"

He was back in the chair, placing a glass ashtray on its arm. He lit a cigarette—Kent, Gavra noticed. American, the preferred brand of all doctors. Arendt said, "Zrinka arrived at the Tarabon clinic a decade ago, back in sixty-five. Fifteen years old. She'd been through a tragedy—both her parents committed suicide. The experience, as you'd imagine, scarred her. She blamed herself."

"She thought she murdered them?" asked Katja.

"In a way, yes. You see, Zrinka believed she had influenced them." He paused, touching his lip, smoke rising into his eyes. "This is going to sound ludicrous to you."

"Go on, Doctor," said Gavra.

He took a drag. "Zrinka Martrich had delusions. In particular, a very strong delusion of 'thought broadcasting,' which means that she believed her thoughts could be heard by other people. The difference between Zrinka and schizophrenics who usually suffer from this was that she didn't believe the people were listening *in*. She wasn't afraid of mental spies or anything like that; she wasn't paranoid. She instead felt that she could speak, with her mind, to other people, and that by doing this she could manipulate people into doing her will."

"So she was crazy," said Katja.

"Well, it wasn't that simple."

"How do you mean?" said Gavra.

The doctor tapped ash and brought his hand to his ear, as if he had trouble hearing. "At first, yes. For the first year she showed characteristics of hysteria, violent panic, and once tried to kill herself. But by the second year she seemed to . . . *adjust.* She stopped displaying the normal characteristics of delusion. Zrinka became completely lucid. Her thoughts were clear; they all made sense. This sort of thing is extremely rare."

"And she left the asylum," said Gavra. "You cured her?"

The doctor took another drag. "I never cured her of her delusions. I tried, many times, but she always maintained her calm. Over the next six years. Six years of weekly talks."

"So why did you let her go?"

"I didn't," he said. "She was transferred to another clinic in seventy-two. It was out of my hands."

Katja sat up. "What other clinic?"

"Rokošyn. It's small, in the mountains. I didn't want her to go, because it's a research institute. Their only interest is observation. Their excuse was that in seven years I'd done nothing for her, so she might as well serve the state. I was unable to keep her."

"What happened to her then?" Katja asked.

The doctor tapped off some ash. "I've checked, but there are no records. The last documents I have are her transfer papers to Rokošyn, from three years ago."

In the silence that followed, Gavra went to the window, looked down into the street, then turned back. The light from the window behind him left his features in darkness. "Would it surprise you if I told you she was spotted in the airport three *days* ago? She made a telephone call to the Hotel Metropol, then boarded a flight to Istanbul."

The doctor's mouth fell open, revealing badly made false teeth. "The one that exploded?"

Gavra looked at Katja; Katja nodded.

"Yes," said Arendt, staring at his thin rug. "It would surprise me."

Gavra came closer. "Did she display any political passions when you knew her?"

He shook his head. "Absolutely none. She was apolitical. I also tried to cure her of this, but . . . well, it's difficult."

"Of course it is."

Katja said, "Does she have any relatives who might know more?"

"Only her brother, but I doubt he knows anything more."

"Brother?"

The doctor nodded. "Yes. Adrian Martrich. I told him about the Rokošyn clinic as well." He noticed their faces. "You didn't know she had a brother?"

PETER

1968

•

There is something comforting about being taken prisoner by amateurs. They make mistakes all the time. Though he realized their mistake quickly, Peter did not at first move. He remained on his cot and listened to the undertones and footsteps in the corridor, trying to ascertain his position here. The sonata came to mind. Themes in a sonata change roles depending on the melodies around them or the key they're in—a light, airy melody becomes ominous in a minor key. Peter had gone from incompetent farm boy to demure, silent music student, then co-conspirator—albeit a minor one—in the making of *socialismu lidskou tvár*. Then, for mere days, he'd been a refugee until, for just a few moments that night in the field outside České Budějovice, he'd become a fool. And that role, like a change in key, had colored the roles that followed. Prisoner, suspect, traitor—and now, fugitive.

Peter climbed out the window and jumped two floors to the bushes below. Bare branches scratched his sore face, but he had no trouble getting up and running through the warm dusk, past unsuspecting students, down Pod Stanicí.

He wasn't sure where to go. His family was in Encs, on the

southern border—but that was no longer his home. His small circle of friends now despised him. So he found himself, after another long tram ride, on Celetná, in front of the Torpédo bar.

Stanislav Klym was already at their back table, but without his rifle. Before him was a full ashtray, a sheet of paper, and three empty beer glasses, a fourth at his lips. He lowered it. "Peter! Come on, come take a seat." Stanislav waved to the bartender for another beer. "What happened to your face?"

"Some trouble."

"Trouble?"

"Some friends."

"Not very friendly."

Peter touched his cheek. "They had reason."

"Did you kill someone?"

"I've made mistakes."

Stanislav grunted. "Haven't we all! But the kinds of friends who beat you to teach a lesson, those are friends you can do without. Here."

The bartender set a fresh glass on the table and, before leaving, caught Peter's eye. It was a hard stare. Stanislav slid the glass to Peter. "Drink up. You're among friends now."

It surprised Peter how comfortable this soldier made him feel. Stanislav was in a mild state of euphoria, waiting for his trip back home. He patted his pocket. "Ticket's here, I've already said good-bye to the regiment, and now I'm going to drink until eight thirty in the morning, when the train leaves. You know what I'm going to do as soon as I get back?"

"What?"

"I'm going to marry my Katja." He tapped the paper in front of him, which Peter now saw was one of her letters. "That's all I'm interested in doing. And then we're going to stay in bed for a week." He folded the letter and slipped it into his pocket. "You ever been in love?"

"I think so."

"What do you mean, you think so?" Stanislav shook his head. "You must not have been, because when you are, you know it."

"I did a lot of things so she would notice me. I abandoned my schoolwork for her. To me, that's love."

"And how far did it get you?"

Peter didn't answer at first. He stared at his glass, then at the soldier's face. He felt a pang of the thing he had felt that whole trip—first in a pickup truck, then on foot—to the Austrian border: jealousy. An intense jealousy that erupted whenever he saw the two of them under their blanket, the way Ivana stroked Toman's cheeks until he fell asleep, and the kisses she woke him with. "It didn't get me far at all. You can see the result here." He touched his pink eye.

"Then you need to stop that."

"Stop what?"

"Doing so much for others. You've got to be independent. Women like that."

"I can't be independent here. Everyone knows me."

"Then get out of Prague," said Stanislav. "Try Bratislava. Start doing things for yourself."

"Once I get some money together, maybe."

The soldier placed a fist on the table. "Don't procrastinate. I've spent enough of my life procrastinating. Now I know what I want. It's my girlfriend, my apartment, and a quiet life. You should go somewhere else. Then no one will disrupt your plans. You can start again, become who you want to be."

It struck Peter that this soldier, unlike himself, did not change key. He had no relation to the sonata. Whether or not he donned a uniform, Stanislav Klym remained what he would always be—a simple man motivated by his love for one woman.

"You sure you're all right?" asked Stanislav.

"Can you excuse me a minute?"

"You're leaving?"

"I just need to make a call. There's a pay phone outside."

"There's a phone behind the bar."

"I'll be right back."

He got up and wound his way through tables and smoke and wide, hunched backs until he was outside. Across the street, two more soldiers shared a cigarette, unaware of him. He walked to the Czech Telecom booth on Republic Square, across from the Obecní Dům, and closed himself inside.

After a minute, the voice spoke to him. "Captain Poborsky here."

"Look at you. You're shivering. It's cold out there?"

"No," said Peter. "Mind getting another round for us?"

Stanislav held up two fingers for the bartender, mouthing *pivo,* then turned back. "You look like you just saw a dead man."

Peter rubbed his arm. "Tell me about your home."

"You don't want to hear about that again."

"I do. Really."

So Stanislav began to speak. When he talked of his grandfather's apartment on 24th of October Street—building number 24, in fact—it was as if he were speaking of a palace. One with limited hot water and peeling walls, but a palace nonetheless. His description of his village, Pácin, was cursory, a few friends and a loyal family, but with one truly extraordinary detail—Katja Uher. They had been in school together, their parents distantly related like everyone in that village. Even though they had spent all their time together, neither of their parents had expected them to fall deeply in love when she was fifteen and he seventeen, but they all condoned it, as if it were as inevitable as the harvest.

"Peter?"

"Yeah?"

"You're not listening."

Peter smiled. "I'm listening to every word. Trust me. Do you have the time?"

The soldier squinted at his watch. "Little after eight."

"Mind if I step out again? Ten minutes?"

Stanislav took the letter out of his pocket again and unfolded it. "Take your time."

GAVRA

•

Doctor Arendt told them what little he knew: that Zrinka Martrich's brother, Adrian, was twenty-three years old, two years younger than her; that he was unmarried, living in the Fourth District; and that he managed the state butcher's shop on Union Street.

Gavra drove while Katja opened the doctor's file on her lap, squinting in the failing light. Beneath the stacks of memos she found a photograph of Zrinka, taken five years ago at the hospital. "Pretty girl," she said.

He glanced over and saw a striking brunette with eyes that in the black-and-white were a very pale gray. "Yeah."

"Do you believe the doctor?"

"It's an elaborate story for a lie."

"I don't trust him," said Katja. "This Zrinka is just swept away to Rokošyn and vanishes? How does that happen?"

Gavra considered his answer, then just gave it. "Katja, people disappear all the time."

On Union Street, they found the butcher's shop where a young man was locking the front door from inside. As they got out of the car and approached, he seemed to be trying to work the key faster, but he stopped when Gavra knocked on the glass. He looked terrified.

"Adrian Martrich?" asked Gavra.

The young man shook his head and said something they couldn't hear.

Gavra pointed at the key. "Open the door." The young man did this.

"We're looking for Adrian Martrich," said Katja.

"Not me. Adrian's in the back."

Gavra put his hand on the door. "Well, then. Take us to him."

He led them past the empty glass cases, in which Gavra noticed traces of blood still not wiped clean, and to a back door. He knocked.

"Yeah?" came a voice.

"Adrian," said the young man, his voice weak, "some people to talk to you."

"Okay," said Adrian Martrich, and they heard papers being put away. By the time the boy had opened the door, Zrinka's brother was at a clean desk. He stood and offered his hand, smiling congenially, as if he'd been expecting their visit.

Gavra felt a choking sensation in the back of his throat. Adrian Martrich was tall and handsome, similar to the way his dead sister was beautiful. As they sat, Gavra grew warm, looking at that well-formed face, pale blue eyes, and thin, coiffed sideburns beneath a wave of brown hair. This man took good care of himself. He looked like no butcher Gavra had ever seen.

From his smile, it appeared that Adrian Martrich wasn't disappointed by what he saw, either.

All this, Gavra knew, should have been a warning.

"Comrade Martrich?" said Katja.

He answered her but continued to look at Gavra. "Yes?"

"We're here to ask about your sister."

Adrian blinked at her. "You know where Zrinka is?"

She began to shake her head but stopped short of lying. "When was the last time you talked to her?"

"Three? Yes, three years ago. When she was in the clinic."

"Tarabon."

He nodded.

"Did your sister have friends in Istanbul?"

"Istanbul?" Adrian snorted lightly. "Not that I know of." Then he looked back at Gavra. "But three years is a long time."

"It certainly is," said Katja. "And you never wondered where she was?"

Adrian Martrich sized her up a moment. "Of course I wondered where she was. Some months ago, her old doctor, Comrade Arendt, sent me to a little town in the countryside. He said she was there. Rokošyn. But when I arrived I realized he was lying."

"Why?"

"Because," he said, "there was nothing there. As far as I know, there's never been a clinic at Rokošyn."

Gavra leaned forward; Katja frowned. She said, "Did you talk to the doctor again after that?"

"Why should I? He obviously wasn't interested in helping me."

Gavra placed a hand on the desk. "Zrinka was on a plane three days ago. It was headed for Istanbul, but it was hijacked and exploded. She's dead."

"Dead?" said Adrian. A nervous smile crossed his face, then vanished. He placed his own hands on the desk, flat. "Zrinka?"

"We're sorry to have to give you this news," Katja said, and followed with words of sympathy, but it was obvious that the butcher was no longer listening. He was staring at his hands.

"You're talking about that plane," he said finally. "The one in the *Spark*. Flight 54."

"Yes," said Gavra, his voice now very soft. "We're trying to find out what your sister was doing on that plane."

Adrian breathed a few times, loudly, then looked at Gavra. "I wish I knew."

Gavra drove again as they headed through the dim streets back to Doctor Arendt. Katja stretched, trying to get rid of the tension of a long day in the car. She said, "Okay. If we believe the brother, then the question: Why did Doctor Arendt tell him, and then us, that Zrinka had been sent to a nonexistent clinic?"

"Because he doesn't want to say where she really went."

The sun was low behind the doctor's Fifth District apartment, and they had to squint to see well. The door to the building was locked, so Katja pressed Arendt's buzzer.

Along the street, families were promenading after early dinners. Katja followed Gavra's gaze and pressed the buzzer again. "They look satisfied, don't they?"

Gavra didn't answer. He was thinking of Adrian Martrich, the handsome butcher.

Then the door opened, but it wasn't the doctor. It was an old woman with a tattered pink babushka tied around her head. When she noticed their dress uniforms, she froze in the doorway, eyes wide.

Katja gave her a smile.

"Potatoes," the old woman said.

"I'm sorry," said Katja. "We don't have potatoes."

The old woman raised a bent finger and pointed across the street to a vegetable shop, and Gavra stepped out of the way. She passed quickly. They caught the door and went inside.

As they took the stairs, they didn't say a thing. It wasn't worth discussing.

Gavra was the one who knocked on the doctor's door. He was the one standing there when it opened on its own, from the pressure of his knuckle. Against the far wall, the open wardrobe spilled files all over the floor, a few covering the doctor, who lay in the middle of his living room, facedown, with a bullet hole in the back of his skull.

PETER

1968

•

He could not walk. The occasional soldier watched him jog past in the darkness, and a few even seemed to consider stopping him, though none did. Soon he was running through vacant streets, the evening humidity choking his nostrils and eyes, so that when he stopped at a doorway not far from where Jungmannova crossed Jungmannovo Square, he could hardly make out the large, flat façade of the Church of Our Lady of the Snows. Through the arched doorway leading from the church courtyard, shapes stumbled out, and beyond the thumping in his head he heard voices. *Come on, you bastards. Hooligans.* The sound of bodies being thrown to the ground. The crack of a truncheon against bone. One scream, but just one. By the time his vision cleared it was a surprisingly quiet scene. Two white trucks and a white Mercedes. Twenty gloomy students. Jan. Gustav. And a black-robed old priest. Josef was probably already inside the trucks the soldiers were leading everyone into.

Peter stepped back, farther into the darkness, and measured out his breaths. It helped to remember that Emperor Charles IV had built this massive church to remind him of his coronation.

What an ego. Despite the humidity, Peter felt the August night turning cold.

When he looked again, the back door of the Mercedes opened, and that man stepped out to light a cigarette. He didn't seem proud, not as proud as he'd seemed in the interrogation room or later in the café. He instead looked like a man at the end of a long day of factory work, the weight of repetitive motion bearing on him. But strong. Bald, tall, and strong.

"Now you look like you've been hit by a train. Where do you keep running off to?"

He tried on a smile as he sat down. "I've had enough beer."

Stanislav folded the letter into his pocket again. "Listen, this is my last night to be foolish. Once I'm back . . . well, I'll have responsibilities. You up for a final blast?"

Peter felt his special talent—the one the StB officer had been so impressed by—bring on a big, authentic smile. "I don't want to let you down."

So they bought a bottle of Becherovka liquor and began again to drink. "Did you fight?" asked Peter.

"When?"

"Here. You've only said you ended up being stationed here. You never told me what you did."

Stanislav shifted, then peered into his shot glass. "Most of the time, no. We were all quite pleased no one wanted to fight us. These girls—pretty girls, and what short skirts they had—they gave us flowers and told us to go home." He shook his head. "As if we had a choice in the matter. But they were nice. At the beginning, though, there was some fighting." He finished his glass and refilled it. "It was the twenty-first. We'd just gotten here, and half of us didn't even know where we were. Then we were sent over to the radio building, over on Stalinova Street. A big crowd outside. I think the radio station had called them all there to protest. Well, it got out of hand. They threw rocks, someone started shooting, and, well . . ." He lifted the dark liquor to his chin. "Yeah, there were dead people."

"Did *you* kill anyone?"

"I hope not. In the confusion, I couldn't tell. But the station—" He grunted. "Those guys are clever. Radio Prague still broadcasts from different areas of town. They change frequencies and give out news for ten minutes, then move on. I doubt anyone will be able to stop them."

"Does that bother you?"

"Me?" Stanislav peered at the dark liquor in his glass. "You think any of us want to be here? You think any of us are here because we want to defend socialism?"

Peter raised his own glass. "To going home."

They swallowed what they had and then poured more.

KATJA

•

As the plane descends toward Atatürk International, I yawn to pop my ears. Beside me, the young electric-fan salesman rubs his eyes and smiles. "Did I sleep the whole way?"

"Yes."

"You?"

"I can't seem to sleep these days."

"Well, you won't sleep in Istanbul. Very unrestful place. Where are you staying?"

His thin hair lies flat on his scalp, and in a few years he'll be bald. He has bright eyes.

"I didn't make a reservation," I say, and it occurs to me how sudden this trip is. How ill planned. This afternoon, taking the long taxi ride from the Hotel Metropol to the airport, fingering my crisp new passport, it felt like the only option. But that was the fatigue confusing me. The fatigue and the buzzing in my ears that muted all other sounds.

"Well, you've got to make a reservation," he says. "It's a popular city. I'm staying at the Pera Palas. Why don't you come into town with me and we'll see if we can get you a room?"

"Yes," I say, trying on a smile. "That's a good idea."

"I'm Istvan. Istvan Farkas."

I make a smile with teeth and take his hand. "Good to meet you, Istvan."

Then I notice the fat man looking at me again. When I catch him he turns away.

Waiting for Brano Sev at the Metropol earlier today, I also felt watched—a woman on her own at the half-empty bar, male eyes converging on my back. So I ordered vodka from a lanky bartender who set the glass down and smiled. "You waiting for someone?"

"Don't give me trouble," I said. He grunted and moved on to another customer.

Brano arrived, sweating in his too heavy jacket, and stubbed out a half-smoked cigarette. He moved quickly for an old man. The bartender, recognizing him, slipped back. "Comrade Sev, so good—"

"Žywiec."

"Of course."

Brano took off his jacket and climbed onto a stool. There were sweat stains all over his shirt. "As I told you on the telephone, Katja, I don't know where Gavra is. He—"

"That's not why I asked you here."

"Okay." The bartender set down a glass of beer and disappeared again. "Then why am I here?"

I took a breath. "Two days ago, on Monday, you and Gavra met a man in the Seventh District, on Tolar. He's young, like me. He has a little mustache now. His name is Peter Husák. Where is he now?"

Brano's face, unused to expressing emotion, let slip an instant of surprise. "Peter Husák?"

"Yes. Where is he?"

"Why are you interested in this man?"

"It's personal."

"Nothing's personal."

I considered my words. With Brano Sev, a misplaced syllable could end all discussion. "I knew him, once. Some years ago. In 1968."

"How well did you know him?"

"He was—" I paused. "He *told* me he was a friend of my old boyfriend. That he knew him in Prague."

"Why was your boyfriend in Prague?"

"He was in the army. He died there. He helped put down their revolution."

"Their counterrevolution."

"Whatever."

"And that's how Peter Husák knew your boyfriend?"

"He told me he worked with our soldiers, that they became close."

"Your boyfriend's name?"

"Stanislav Klym."

Brano touched his glass but didn't lift it. He nodded. "Right."

"What?"

He stood up. "I have to go now, but . . ." He frowned, considering something. "Can you meet me back here at five?"

"Yes."

"Okay. I'll see you at five."

Then he was gone.

GAVRA

•

Brano Sev arrived looking as he always did. Unamused. He stared at Arendt's body, the blood that matted his once-white hair and soaked the rug, then turned to Katja. "Comrade Drdova, would you please interview the neighbors? I saw a few venturing out. Statements might be of use."

Katja looked at Gavra, who shrugged. She marched out.

Brano spoke quietly. "So?"

"We interviewed the doctor earlier," Gavra said. "We learned that Zrinka Martrich was delusional. She spent time in the Vuz-love clinic—Tarabon—but was transferred three years ago to Rokošyn, a research institute."

"Rokošyn?"

"Yes. But the brother—her brother, Adrian Martrich—claims this is a lie, because there's no clinic in Rokošyn. While we were interviewing the brother, someone did this."

"Adrian Martrich is right," said Brano. "There hasn't been a clinic in Rokošyn for years. There was, but it was shut down long ago."

Gavra raised Zrinka Martrich's file. "The killer made a mess, probably looking for this."

"I see."

"I want to talk to Adler again."

Brano squatted beside the doctor. He used the flat end of a pencil to look inside Arendt's pants pockets. "I wouldn't worry about Wilhelm Adler. His wife returned home an hour ago and found him in the living room, much like the doctor here."

"Dead?" Gavra muttered, but Brano didn't bother answering. He walked to the front door and began examining the frame for forced entry, while Gavra tried to manage his annoyance. "Adler's killed because he talked to us," said Gavra. "So it's what I thought. The Ministry's involved."

Again, Brano Sev didn't answer.

"You know something about this, don't you? Where's Ludvík Mas?"

Brano maintained his silence as he walked to the window, pulled back the curtain, and peered down at the dark street, now empty of promenading families. "A funeral and two murders." He let the curtain go. "It's been a long day."

Gavra threw Zrinka Martrich's file on the desk. "Why aren't you helping?"

"I'll see what I can do."

"What does that mean?"

"Are you watching the brother?" said Brano. "This Adrian Martrich?"

"I will."

"Give Katja the first shift. You need sleep."

"I'm fine."

"That's an order. And Gavra?"

"Yes?"

"Be sure and have your pistol next time. I can see you're un-armed."

"Oh. Right."

Brano Sev walked out.

Katja returned, predictably, with nothing from the neighbors. She'd knocked on doors, and the few who chose to answer insisted they had just returned home or had been watching the evening repeat of *Family Popa* and heard nothing. So Gavra told her about Adler's murder.

"Jesus," she said.

"Can you watch Adrian Martrich's apartment? The Comrade insists I get some sleep."

"No problem," she said, then looked at the wet rug and added, half to herself, "Better than going home."

Gavra had a natural affinity for puzzles, but this one wouldn't fit together. Two murders in the Capital and a terrorist action gone wrong. The only connection was a young woman, Zrinka, who had died on the plane, a delusional who left a message for the terrorists when they were standing in the same terminal she was. Zrinka's old therapist was dead, as well as the German who helped arrange the hijacking.

The answer was in there, he knew, but his Yalta-trained logic was of no use. So he floundered, rolling in his musty bed, finally going to the kitchen for the palinka, which only did its job at 3:00 A.M.

He nearly made it out the door without his Makarov, and had to run back to the bedroom to search for his shoulder holster. He relieved Katja at ten, by which time she'd followed Adrian Martrich in her Škoda from his apartment to the tram, and then to Union Street—where, it appeared, Martrich had decided to open for a few Sunday hours in honor of the next day's holiday, Monday the twenty-eighth of April, General Secretary Tomiak Pankov's birthday.

Katja had nothing to report because she was tired—she admitted to falling asleep a few times in the car. Gavra was too exhausted to practice intimidation with her.

After she drove off, he settled in his own Škoda across the street from the butcher shop. It was warm out, so he'd worn shirtsleeves under his jacket, and now loosened his tie. He spent the next few hours trying not to sleep.

During the past year under Brano Sev's tutelage, he'd sat in so many cars on so many street corners, simply watching. At first it was nearly impossible to take. He grew bored and fidgety within the first half hour and always had to pee. He'd limp off to an alleyway to relieve himself, glancing around the corner to be sure his subject hadn't changed position, then hurry back to sit behind the wheel. For daytime watches, he found it helped to bring along a novel. He'd read *Anna Karenina* during a weeklong session last summer, and remembered being pleased when Tolstoy entered the mind of a hunting dog as easily as he entered Anna's.

But Brano disapproved of reading on the job and forced him to learn to do without his books. *Mental quiet,* his tutor said. *Like the Buddhists.*

What do you know about Buddhism?

A woman I loved used to be a Buddhist.

Gavra couldn't imagine Brano with either a woman or a man. Who, after all, could fall for someone as cold as that? The advice was sound though. Sitting in his car, Gavra silenced his wandering thoughts and watched Adrian Martrich come out now and then to oversee the mute crowds their country produced whenever a fresh shipment of lamb arrived. The line grew the length of the block. Gavra observed with some detached interest the subculture of the queue—how, with time, a straight line becomes a crowd, and then each person takes a role. A tall, older man becomes the dictator, keeping track of the order, stopping one person and letting one through. Another, perhaps an old woman, becomes his assistant, her careful eye on everyone, tugging the dictator's sleeve at the first sign of disruption. Among the sheep are the gossipers, the knitters, the readers, as well as the complainers who make speeches to strangers about the infiltrator—usually a Gypsy who ignores the painstakingly arranged order and tries to slip in undetected. But he never succeeds, because the assistant has tugged the dictator's sleeve; the dictator has spoken and pointed; and the infiltrator has been blocked by a wall of firm backs, shoulder to shoulder, these steadfast sheep acting as if there's no one behind them, trying to get through.

Gavra watched until four, when the meat ran out and Martrich walked the length of the block, asking everyone to please leave. Adrian carried himself very well among his disappointed customers. He patted their shoulders and bent to speak with very old, shrunken women. He knew them all and treated them as if they were his people. And they, Gavra could see, appreciated this. They appreciated him. They liked this handsome, pale-eyed young man who handed them their daily ration of meat.

An hour later Gavra watched Adrian's young assistant leave for home, then Adrian himself locked up. He paused at the door, looking up the street toward the tram stop at the next intersection. He ran his fingers through his hair.

Then Adrian Martrich turned, smiled directly at Gavra, and crossed the street to meet him.

Gavra rolled down his window; Adrian bent close.

"Comrade Noukas, you're not trying to be secretive, are you?"

"Uh, no." Gavra's mental silence was breaking up.

"I noticed Comrade Drdova out here earlier, too. You don't think I blew up my sister's plane, do you?"

Adrian was becoming irritating, but Gavra had the overwhelming sense that he was doing this on purpose. "Just making sure you're all right."

"Very comforting," said Adrian. "If you're watching anyway, can you give me a lift home? Save tram fare."

Gavra wasn't sure how Brano would feel about this, but there was no point letting the old man know. "Come on."

They drove north along empty Sunday streets, and while Gavra tried not to look at his passenger, he felt Adrian's presence; the right half of his body began to sweat.

"Why do I need protection?"

"We're not sure you need it."

"But you have reason to worry."

"Yes."

"Doctor Arendt?"

Gavra submitted and looked at him. "How did you know that?"

Adrian was staring straight ahead through the windshield. "Lucky guess. Is he dead?"

"Yes."

"Why?"

"I don't know," said Gavra. "Do you?"

Adrian shook his head. "You think it has something to do with Zrinka?"

"I'm not sure."

"Don't know much, do you?" He didn't say this with any bitterness, and Gavra didn't bother answering.

When they parked in the vast gravel lot between apartment blocks, Adrian said, "Might as well come up. You'll fall asleep down here."

Gavra knew what his mentor would say to that. "I'll talk to you later."

"You won't fall asleep, then? I mean, if I'm in danger."

"No."

Adrian nodded, then climbed out. Gavra watched him walk gingerly to the glass door of his building and open it with a key. Before entering, Adrian turned back and shot him another smile.

Gavra lit a cigarette.

He watched neighbors arrive. Old men and women, a group of three teenagers lighting cigarettes, a family with two young children. Everyone appeared tired, returning from long Sunday lunches that inevitably grew into drunken dinners with lascivious uncles, dozing fathers, fussy mothers, and grandmothers cooking vast meals for dozens. Gavra remembered them from childhood as wonderful, exhausting affairs, where he would run around his grandparents' farm with a pellet gun, shooting crows perched on branches. But he'd never known those Sunday lunches as an adult, because after joining the Ministry he had never returned home. He sometimes considered visiting—surely by now he had no reason to be uncomfortable there. He was an adult, and an officer of the Ministry for State Security.

Besides, it was so long ago that his father found him in his grandparents' barn with that young farmhand from Krosno. Gavra had been sixteen then; fourteen years was a long time for any father to sustain his anger.

He'd lost his mental silence, and because of that he nearly missed it when, around six thirty, as the shadows of the occasional tree stretched across the glass entryway, an old Saxon walked up to the front door, fumbling with his keys, then stopped. The old man looked back as a younger man in a wide hat jogged up, calling for him to wait. From his open window, Gavra could hear the peculiar accent of the jogger. Flat, the syllables spoken from the front of the mouth.

Western. Perhaps American.

The old man noticed it, too, his surprise evident even from this distance, but let the man in with him as Gavra threw his cigarette out the window.

Gavra didn't open the door, because there were perhaps eighty apartments in Zrinka's brother's ten-story building, making a total of at least two hundred inhabitants. There was no reason to assume this foreigner had arrived to see Adrian Martrich. So he hesitated, just a few seconds, until another man jogged across the pitted courtyard and used a key to get inside.

The man's suit was too tight, and an air of claustrophobia surrounded him.

Gavra climbed out of his car and began to run, because that second man was Ludvík Mas.

PETER

1968

•

They were the only customers left in the bar when it closed at one, and they stumbled arm in arm down Celetná, past soldiers standing against the old town's medieval stone walls. Stanislav sometimes drunkenly saluted them. "Oblov, you're still here?" he called in Russian.

A fat soldier on the opposite corner squinted. "Stanislav, get your ass out of my district or I'll personally take care of that girl-friend of yours!"

Stanislav shot him a rude hand gesture, then grabbed Peter's shoulder and walked on.

By the time they reached the arch of the Charles Bridge's Old Town gate, Stanislav was failing. A long day of drinking had broken up his words into barely comprehensible syllables. "Got to . . . I'm . . . uh . . . tired."

"You're tired?"

"*Da.*"

"Should I get you to the train station?"

"No . . . *nyet.* There."

Stanislav pointed at the small door on the inside of the bridge's gate. "In there," he mumbled. "Good for sit."

Peter was surprised to find the battered old door unlocked. Inside in the darkness, he squinted to make out the twisting stone steps leading high into the tower. He peered back to see Stanislav falling through the door, then closing it behind himself. "I don't think you'll make it," said Peter.

"Eh?"

"To the top." He pointed up into the blackness.

"I'll make it." Stanislav ushered him up with his hands.

But as they reached the fourth narrow window that looked down on the bridge and across to the castle district, Stanislav sat heavily on a step.

"Just a little . . . rest. *Da?* But you . . ." He yawned and looked up. "But you will wake me? Eight," he said. "Eight thirty."

"I'll do that."

Stanislav stifled another yawn and closed his eyes. "You won't . . . sleep?"

Peter settled on a step above the soldier and opened the window, letting in a cool river breeze. The alcohol had been washed away by his night's act of betrayal, and as his eyes adjusted to the shadows of the bridge he wished they'd brought along another bottle. "Don't worry. I won't sleep."

For a half hour Peter remained there, his knees up to his chest. The breeze coming in off the Vltava seeped through his thin coat and pants. From below he heard occasional distant voices he thought were Russian. Once, a truck rumbled across the bridge, and he watched its lights dwindle between the rows of statues.

"What're you thinking, Peter?" Stanislav seemed to be speaking in his sleep.

"I'm wondering how I can have a life like yours."

The soldier squirmed into a tighter fetal position, his head on the step just below Peter's foot. "*Da, da.* Well, wake me up when you know."

Another truck passed under them, then the noise faded away. He had no answers. The only sure thing was that he could not return to the university. His phone call to Captain Poborsky had ended that. Those who had not been rounded up would know who had turned them in. They would manhandle him from his bed in the night, then carry him to some vacant janitor's closet or toilet stall; they would teach him a lesson.

The soldier began to snore. In the darkness, Peter could just see his hunched back, the way he was rolled tight. On the crest of his hip, where his fine coat had fallen back, the knife from his father was looped in his belt. It seemed to Peter like a motif in their relationship. A single object that signified the difference between the two of them. Stanislav's loving family was in that knife, and the knife, like the family, protected Stanislav as he made his way through the world.

Peter cleared his throat. "Stanislav?"

The snores continued, the soldier's chest rising and falling.

Peter spoke quietly. "You wouldn't believe what I've done. I killed my best friend and the woman I loved. Not on purpose, but because of my stupidity. But now—now I'm not so sure. Did I mean to do it? Did I want us to be caught? Was I so jealous I'd rather they were dead than together? Because afterward I did something completely consciously. I made a phone call I never thought I would make. And right now, my old friends are in that convent on Bartolomějská. They're probably . . ." He couldn't finish the sentence aloud, but his mind repeated it in full: *They're probably being tortured.* He cleared his throat again, his mind now inventing grotesque scenes that took place in that small basement room. Poor meek Jan in a chair, tied down, his glasses cracked and blood dripping from his fingernails.

He felt like he was going to be sick, so he put his face as far through the window as he could, sucking in fresh air.

It wasn't only the gore of his imagination, but also the realization of this fact: Because his old friends were the kind of men they were, with their pride and convictions, at some point Comrade Poborsky would walk them out to the convent courtyard and shoot them in the head.

He looked out at the river and across to the lights of the castle district. That was something he would miss. Mistakes or not, what he'd done in the last days had rerouted his life. It was entirely different.

He sank back on the steps, his stomach now settling.

The only sounds were water lapping medieval stones down below and Stanislav's irregular snores. Peter leaned forward and reached out, touching the handle of the knife. Another hawk was carved into its worn wooden handle, stretched to fit the length. When he slid it out, the blade reflected a distant street lamp into his eyes, and he blinked. It was a heavy knife, and well balanced. Like the soldier's family, he thought, and smiled. Because not even then did he know what he was going to do.

In his study of the semantics of music, he had learned about Ferdinand de Saussure's concept of the "dyadic sign," that which unites a work's concept with its sound-image. What Peter liked about this was that it completely disregarded the composer, who, at the point when his work is being played, is entirely disassociated from the piece. His intentions and desires no longer matter. The piece he has written is now simply action and sound. Now, here, Peter felt like a composer out of touch with his creation; he was instead in the audience, only understanding his actions as they were being performed.

He took two steps down and bent over the snoring soldier's large ear. The Warsaw Pact collar was up over the neck, so he folded it down. The soldier did not stir, his snores a steady engine echoing lightly up the tower's stairwell.

By now he knew, though to put it into words would have been impossible. He lowered the knife in front of the soldier's throat, parallel to the ground, and placed a knee behind the neck.

Peter remained in that position for a minute, his quick breaths feeling hot in this cool place.

Only now could he find the words to describe what he was doing.

KATJA

•

What did I do between noon and five, waiting for my second meeting with Brano Sev? That was just five hours ago, but standing here by the carousel, waiting for Istvan Farkas to collect his baggage and feeling naked beside a group of women covered in black with only slits to reveal their eyes, I'm having trouble remembering. Yes—I walked. I walked from the Metropol, up Mihai Boulevard, along the concrete landing that borders the Tisa, stopping to look now and then at the high cranes leaning over the broken roofs of the Canal District. Tomiak Pankov's celebrated project to clean, scour, and rebuild that oldest part of the Capital meant nothing to me. Then I turned onto the small side streets and found a bakery with a few rolls left in the window, eating them as I continued westward, unable to look at the people I passed. This troubled me, that I could not relegate the events of seven years ago—relegate Peter Husák—to a small room in my head, a small room that could be managed and dealt with constructively. Instead, I was left numb, standing at the edge of Victory Park with half-eaten rolls that I let fall to the grass. I worried that the memory of Peter Husák was killing me. I even considered finding Aron and talking to him. After three years of marriage, perhaps, I could finally tell my husband the story that made me cold in bed and ruptured any chance we had of marital calm, or children. But the secret had gone on too long, and now not even honesty could save us.

Once we've bought Turkish lira at an exchange desk and then purchased visas, Istvan says, "Ready?" When he smiles, it's a trembling, proud smile, as if he's hiding a present behind his back. Or a triumphant smile. With only a few words, he's gotten a woman to come to his hotel with him.

We take a taxi through the dry evening fields surrounding Atatürk International, the static of the driver's radio broken now and then by Istvan's innocuous observations: "It's lucky we met, isn't it? . . . You haven't had a *gyro* until you've had one here . . . There's an excellent bar at the hotel, so we can have a decent nightcap."

The main roads take us through European Istanbul, toward a place the signs call Beyoğlu, and the old city grows around us. Istvan points to the right, into a dark spread of lights and roofs that dwindle toward a glowing dome with six pointed spires. "*Sultan Ahmet Camii,*" he says, and the driver perks up.

"*Evet,*" he says, then switches to English: "Blue Mosque. You tourist?"

I nod in the direction of the lights but am distracted by my own reflection in the window.

We cross a bridge, and I say, "This is the Bosphorus?"

"The Golden Horn," Istvan corrects. He again points to the right. "The Bosphorus is over in that direction; on the other side is Asia."

"Asia," I say.

"You're on the very edge of the continent."

When we finally arrive at the Hotel Pera Palas, I'm stunned. It's an enormous, lavish structure, lit up like a church. Under the high ceiling, the marbled lobby is full of grandiose columns and velvet carpets. Men in suits and ties sit in formally arranged leather chairs and read newspapers, sipping tea from glass cups.

The clerk remembers Istvan from a previous visit. "Mister Farkas, we have been expecting you," he says in English.

Istvan glances back at me with a smile—I'm to be impressed. "Good to be back. Perhaps you have a spare room for my friend?"

"Reservation?"

I open my mouth, but Istvan says, "I'm afraid not."

The clerk, whose mustache looks like it was stolen from a much larger man, makes a face, then shrugs dramatically. "If only I could. There is a convention in town—*Greeks,*" he whispers.

"Is that so?"

"I am afraid, yes."

"It's no problem," I say, because a part of me has been wishing that circumstances would stop me at some point and force me to return. Not that I don't want to go through with this, only that I'm searching for some sign, some direction.

Istvan holds up a finger, asking for my patience. He signs a piece of paper and takes his keys, then steps back to me. "I don't know how you feel about it, but my rooms are always too large. They treat me well. And so, if you're not concerned for your safety, I'd be honored if you would stay in my room. There's a large couch for me to sleep on."

"I couldn't."

"It's up to you," he says, leaning close. "But rest assured that this is no inconvenience for me. In fact, it would be a pleasure."

Despite the surprising aura of shoddy decay above the ground floor, our room is in fact two decomposing rooms, a bedroom and a living room. I pull back the curtains and find a terrace that overlooks nighttime Istanbul, the barrage of lights and sounds drifting up to us. When I tell him it's beautiful, he nearly blushes. "I'm lucky the comrades feel their salesmen should maintain an air of sophistication. Do you feel like a drink?"

I'm standing out on the shallow terrace, wondering which of those lights is Peter Husák.

"The bar's just downstairs."

I turn back and give him a smile. "Just let me wash up first."

GAVRA

•

Gavra buzzed a whole row of apartments on the large panel by the front door. A cacophony of puzzled who's-theres sputtered out as he tugged the handle, waiting for that one innocent to let him in. Then he flew through the foyer and up the stairwell, pausing on the second floor, where the dead stranger with the wide hat and the foreign accent lay, blood pulsing from a hole in his trachea. Gavra sprinted on.

On the third floor, looking up to the fourth, he spotted Mas at the top of the stairs with a pistol lengthened by a long silencer screwed to the end of it.

"Ludvík Mas!" he shouted.

Mas looked down, perhaps surprised, his comical mustache twitching.

Gavra raised his Makarov. "Put it on the floor and walk down here."

A trace of a smile flickered across Mas's face. He aimed between Gavra's eyes and descended a step, speaking calmly. "Comrade Noukas, we can both die on this stairwell, or we can both survive the night."

He descended two more steps. He said, "I suggest you speak with Comrade Sev before you pull that trigger."

"Who's the man downstairs?"

"You'll find out soon enough."

He was two steps above Gavra, their pistols pointed at each other's faces. Ludvík Mas lowered his, but Gavra didn't shift his aim.

"I'm going now, Comrade Noukas."

"You're going to tell me what's going on."

"I'll do no such thing. Speak with your superiors." He paused, then added, "Faggot."

He passed quickly, trotted down the next flight, and was gone.

Gavra stood with his gun by his side, feeling suddenly cold, then continued up. In answer to his knock, Adrian opened the door. The butcher's face, at first hesitant, lit up and even smiled when he registered who his visitor was. But Gavra only said, "I need to use your phone."

During the twenty minutes they waited for Brano Sev, Gavra smoked three cigarettes. Adrian poured them each a vodka and sat across from him on the sofa. Absently, Gavra said, "Thanks," and threw back the shot.

"You're sure he's dead?" asked Adrian.

Gavra looked at him.

"From the door," he explained. "I could hear everything."

He nodded.

"Who is he?"

That question stunned him, because in his distraction he

hadn't thought to check this. He bolted out of the apartment. His feet clattered down the stairs. After a few minutes, he returned with a wallet and a passport, frowning. He sat again in the chair and asked Adrian, "Do you know a Maxwell Palmer?"

Adrian shook his head. "Can I see?"

Gavra showed him the bland photo in Maxwell Palmer's passport. The face was also unfamiliar, but Adrian frowned at the cover. "Why is there a dead American here?"

He wanted to be open with Adrian Martrich, to let him know that the man who killed the American was a state security officer, and that he suspected the next target had been Adrian himself— but Ludvík Mas's confidence made this difficult. Mas was part of that shadowy world of the back offices of Yalta, like Room 305, the source of puzzling commands and sudden bursts of retribution. Room 305 was the last office Gavra wanted causing him trouble.

So he held his tongue until Brano Sev arrived, the gray hair behind his ears wet, as if he'd been called from the bath. He nodded imperceptibly at Adrian, then turned to Gavra. "Comrade Noukas, can we talk?"

In the corridor and down the stairs, Gavra told him every detail of the story, omitting only Mas's final word, *faggot.*

Brano looked through the dead American's papers. "So it's Maxwell Palmer tonight."

"You know him?"

"His real name is Timothy Brixton, CIA. His cover is as a television salesman." Brano paused. "What was Brixton doing here?"

"He came alone, and an old man let him in."

"A contact?"

"No. But Ludvík Mas was following him. And he had a key."

"He would."

Brano squatted to stare at the hole in the dead American's throat. Blood covered Brixton's clothes and congealed on the stairs. Gavra could still smell the potassium nitrate from the shot that had killed him.

"You say Mas was heading to Adrian Martrich's apartment?"

"Looks that way. But when he saw me, he left. It seems clear enough that Ludvík Mas also murdered Doctor Arendt and Wilhelm Adler, and that his next target was Adrian Martrich."

"Is it clear?" Brano began going through the dead American's pockets. "But Timothy Brixton was here for a reason as well."

"Are you going to talk to Mas?"

"I'll certainly try," said Brano.

"He's our prime suspect."

Brano came up with some loose change and a key from the Hotel Metropol.

"Can you tell me?" Gavra asked.

"I can't tell you what I don't know."

"Mas seemed to think you would know."

Brano stood. "I can find out. Let's get someone to clean this up. And, Gavra?"

"Yes?"

"Keep this quiet. It's not the kind of thing Katja should know about." Brano handed over the Metropol key and squinted at the top of the stairs as something occurred to him.

"What?"

Brano shook his head. "We'll talk more tomorrow. Just make sure Comrade Martrich survives the night."

KATJA

•

We're on velvet-seated stools at the Orient Express Bar of the Pera Palas, surrounded by pink-tinted walls. Past Istvan, at dark corner tables, men in loosened ties with fuming cigarettes huddle over drinks, and the occasional tourist family tries to rein in their children. This is so different from the bar where I last met Brano Sev.

"Spies used to come here," says Istvan.

"That so?"

"Mata Hari, Kim Philby. Back when spying was still glamorous." He winks when he says that, and, as he slides a glass with clear liquor in front of me, adds, "Agatha Christie wrote *Orient Express* in one of their rooms."

"Thus the name of this bar."

"Exactly."

I look at my glass as he pours cold water into it, the mix turning milky.

"*Rakı,* Turkish brandy," he says. "Is that all right?"

I answer by draining the anise-heavy liquid, and Istvan, seemingly impressed, calls for another.

He talks to me like a man trying to sell something. He tells me about electric fans. "The real symbol of the twentieth century. Man over nature. When nature makes you hot, you beat her to the ground with one of these. The next step is climatization, what the Americans call 'air-conditioning,' but we're not yet ready for that much control over nature."

"You're very philosophical for a salesman."

"You'd be surprised. Salesmen are some of the most philosophical people around. It's the long hours alone, stuck with your own thoughts. And the hotels, which, even if they're as beautiful as this one, begin to look the same. The world begins to look the same. And you start to wonder how different we all really are, and why we do what we do. That's really all of philosophy in a nutshell."

"The *why*."

"Yes, *why*. That's the basic question of philosophy. *How* is a question for science."

"Maybe you should write this down."

"I know my limits." He takes a drink and cocks his head, and in this light I can see his scalp through his thin hair. "So why are you in Istanbul? Obviously not business, or you'd have a reservation."

"I just wanted to see it. Istanbul."

"And what do you do back in the Capital?"

I'm not sure at first if I should answer, but then it seems that there have been too many secrets around me, and I don't want this to continue. "I'm a militiawoman."

Istvan inhales, bobbing impressed eyebrows. "I'd never have guessed."

"Why not?"

He answers as if he's standing behind a podium. "From my experience you can tell the Militia type pretty quickly. They walk
like they're being watched all the time. They give off this silent-
but-judging aura they want everyone to notice. As if what's going
on in their heads is for them, and only them, to know about."

"Isn't everyone like that?"

"You're not."

I smile, lean closer. "Then tell me what I'm like."

He peers at me over the rim of his glass, his eyes twinkling—
he likes this. "Well, you're average height, so you don't stand out
that way. You're not overly muscled, which would also stand out
on a woman. But you're fit. That could mean any sort of job."

"You're just describing my body."

"Have to start somewhere. So . . . you do have a habit of taking
in a place when you enter. Like this bar. When we came in, you
immediately looked to your left and right, to see what was on either side of the door. Usually people look ahead, to where they
want to end up. But you're careful." He shrugs. "I suppose that's
the training."

I sip my *rakı* and wait for more.

"You know how you look," he says. "In that way you're self-
conscious. But not in the way most militiamen are. You're self-
conscious the way beautiful women are. They know that when
they enter a room, eyes will turn to them. They know that because of this they have some power."

"You're embarrassing me."

"I'm just telling you what I see. When we were on the plane
and I started to speak with you, you acted as if I were asking for
your phone number. Because you're used to this. So you went out
of your way to ignore me, even though I was sitting next to you."

"I'm sorry," I say, because at that moment I really am.

"I'm not offended; it's a common thing. It's how beautiful women protect themselves. Why should they have to lose their anonymity just because of the way they look? It's unfair, so you have to fight it." He looks down at my empty glass. "You want another?"

"Water," I say, and he orders this from the bartender, as well as another *rakı* for himself. Then he measures me with his eyes.

"Now that you tell me you're a militiawoman, it starts to make me wonder. In France I've run into a couple of policewomen, but they tend to shape themselves into men. Short haircuts, a kind of forced machismo. Partly so that the public will take them seriously; partly so their co-workers will stop trying to kiss them. But your fingernails—you keep them painted and long. Your hair is well cared for. And you use makeup."

I instinctively touch my cheek.

"You must have a difficult time in the Militia office. What department?"

"I'm a homicide inspector."

He takes another breath, very affected. "Now, that's interesting. What made you want to track down murderers?"

No one has ever asked me that before, so I don't have a pat answer ready. I've only been asked, by my worried family, why I'd want to work with Militia oafs—and by my frustrated husband, why I'd want to risk my life. But homicide in particular?

It's the same reason I'm here in Istanbul.

I say, "Some years ago, my fiancé was murdered."

"Did they catch his killer?"

I shake my head.

"So you do this in order to avenge him."

"Perhaps."

He drinks his *rakı* and considers that. "What about the abstract stuff?"

"What?"

"The state—defending the order of the state and all that?"

"Of course. That, too."

"But not really."

I pause, then shake my head.

He takes another sip. "What if he was caught? The murderer, I mean. Let's say you caught him and he was sent to some work camp. Let's say he's sent to dig the Canal. What would you do?"

"I'd be happy."

"But would you want to leave your job?"

"I don't follow."

He smiles. "It's simple, Katja. If he's the reason you wanted to become a homicide inspector, and you took care of that reason, would you still want to be a homicide inspector?"

I can feel myself flushing, because I don't like this question. It sounds too much like a question Aron might pose. *If you left the Militia, would you then have my baby?* But I know the answer to this what-if. "I don't know how to be anything else," I say, though I'm not sure he believes me. I'm not sure I believe myself.

PETER

1968

•

He rubbed his eyes and gazed out the dirty window at the passing countryside, rubbing the scratches on the back of his hand. Flat fields had given way to rolling hills under an overcast late-morning sky. Across from him in the compartment was a fat farmer's wife, not unlike his own mother, her babushka tied tightly under her chin. She ate pumpkin seeds and tried not to stare at the blood soaked into the upturned collar of his army jacket.

He'd slept the whole way from Prague, then been woken in Šarišske by a Czech border guard, who, though he noticed the blood, was too intimidated by the uniform to comment. Peter handed over Stanislav Klym's documents with a serious expression and accepted them back just as morbidly. It was in Šarišske that this woman had joined him.

He hadn't thought about the blood when he plunged the knife into Stanislav Klym's neck. He had simply followed what he knew was the inevitable next step. He pushed it through the skin, and when it hit resistance the neck slid back against his knee. The soldier's eyes and mouth snapped open, but without voice. Just the wet rasping of impossible breaths. His fingers came up, clawing

Peter's hands, and his legs kicked. Then Peter let go of the knife and fell back, climbing backward up to the window. It took a minute, maybe two, for the soldier to die. He writhed on the ground as a black pool grew in front of him and dribbled down the steps.

The train slowed and pulled into Velky Saris. On the platform, the men who guarded the border of Peter's new home gathered and approached the train.

He'd stared at the dead soldier a long time, squatting until the balls of his feet burned. He'd wanted to cry but calmed himself by putting his mind elsewhere, into an oral examination he had taken months and another life ago, where he had mistaken the structure of the sonata allegro form—the first theme, followed by a transition into the second theme in a new key. This theme is developed, and then comes the recapitulation—a repeat of the first theme. Then the second theme returns, but in the original key, and is followed by the coda.

How could he have gotten this wrong?

He'd stood when he thought he could do so without falling. Then, despite the chill, he undressed.

"Papers."

He looked up at a young guard in a smart blue uniform with the national symbol of the hawk on its shoulder. The guard bowed his head to the woman as he took her passport. "How are the cows, Irina?"

She shrugged. "Norbert had to shoot the two best ones."

"Oh?" The soldier stamped the passport and handed it back.

"Tuberculosis." She shrugged again. "It happens."

The guard nodded with sympathy, then smiled at Peter as he accepted his papers. "Coming from Prague?"

"I am."

He flipped absently through the passport. "How's it going up there?"

Peter wasn't sure how to answer, and his hesitation earned a look from the guard. "It's improving," he said quickly, then shook his head. "Last week was hell."

The guard pointed at Peter's collar. "Yeah. It looks like it was."

Peter touched the blood. "Earned this at the radio station. I'm lucky to get back with my life."

The woman crossed herself.

"A lucky man," said the guard. He squinted at the photograph in the passport. "You need to start eating."

"You think so?"

"You've lost a lot of weight." He showed the picture to the woman, who nodded her agreement.

"You'll get sick," she said as the guard stamped the passport and handed it back.

"My girlfriend will fatten me up," said Peter. He slipped the passport into his jacket pocket, beside the stiff hunting knife marked by a hawk similar to the one on the guard's shoulder patch.

He'd acquired so much in the past six hours that what he'd lost was barely a memory. Like a simple melody line that gains chords, a variety of keys, and counterpoint, developing into a grand piece, he had acquired a name, a knife, money, and an apartment. In the space of six hours he'd acquired a life.

The guard saluted Peter. "Welcome home, comrade."

KATJA

.

"A *militiawoman*," Istvan says once we're back upstairs. He's in the bedroom, and I'm in the bathroom, removing makeup in the mirror. "You're not on a case, are you?"

"I've got no authority outside our lovely country."

"I see," he says, then stands in the doorway. "You're a very beautiful woman."

I can see him in the reflection, and my face is up close. Perhaps he's right—I have the requisite cheekbones, blond hair, dark eyes—but age is setting in early and I'm wondering what I'll look like at thirty, thirty-five. I'll look fifty, I know it. "It's a temporary beauty," I tell him.

"Where do you want to sleep?"

"In the bed."

His smile is huge.

"And you'll be a gentleman and take the sofa."

He retains the smile another few seconds, but that's only decorum. "Of course, of course. You want another drink? There's a minibar in the cabinet."

"I'm really tired."

"It'll help you sleep."

I stop fooling with my face and turn to look at him. "Really, Istvan. Thanks, but all I want now is a proper rest."

When I come out, he's lying on the sofa in the other room, and I tell him good night as I close the adjoining doors. His *Good night* sounds distinctively frustrated.

Before turning off the light, I call down to the front desk and ask in stilted, stumbling English if they have a reel-to-reel tape player in the hotel. "I believe we do, *bayan*."

"I can use tomorrow?"

"Of course, *bayan*. What time?"

I returned to the Metropol bar an hour before my appointment with Brano Sev because I couldn't stand the sunlight anymore. How can I explain it? The sunlight wasn't a metaphor for anything. No. There are no metaphors in life, simply things. Things that undermine you or give you strength. The sunlight undermined me.

I drank two waters and was rude to one bearded man who tried to start a conversation. Disappointed, he returned to his dim corner table and watched from a distance.

Brano arrived at precisely five. Under his arm was a bulky envelope that he placed on the bar as he climbed onto his stool. He asked the bartender for a beer.

"Comrade Drdova."

"Comrade Sev."

He looked at the glass the bartender placed before him. "Comrade Drdova, this man you call Peter Husák no longer goes by that name. He was . . . well, he came to my attention in 1968, the year you knew him. But when I met him, he wasn't using that name. He went by the name Stanislav Klym."

Up until then I'd had my elbow on the table, my forehead resting in a palm. I dropped my hand slowly. "He used my Stanislav's name?"

"This is why he came to my attention. The real Stanislav Klym had proved himself brave and steadfast during the troubles in Czechoslovakia, an intelligent young man, and I wanted to recruit him. I didn't know, at the time, that he had died in Prague."

"Recruit him for what?"

"For the kind of work I do."

I waited.

"Once I learned Stanislav had returned from Prague, I visited his apartment and found this man who answered to his name. I made the offer of work, and he accepted." Brano took a sip of his beer, then set it down. "The truth came out later, during a week-long interview session. It's something we do to new recruits. We talk with them intensely over the space of a week to be sure they are the kind of people we can work with. This Husák was an adept liar—quite talented, you could say—but over days I began to see that elements of his story didn't fit together. He knew nothing about Pácin, your and Stanislav's hometown, and he could not accurately piece together his time in Czechoslovakia." Brano shrugged. "So the truth finally came out. His real name was the one he gave you, Peter Husák, and he was a Slovak from the border region, which explained why he knew our language so well. He'd gotten into trouble during the counterrevolution and assumed your boyfriend's identity in order to escape the country."

"But," I began, then paused. I looked in my bag until I found a cigarette, then stuck it in my mouth. I didn't light it. "You mean he stole his papers off a dead man?"

Brano took a lighter from his pocket and lit my cigarette for me. He watched me suck on it. "Peter Husák killed Stanislav Klym. For his papers."

His face, through the smoke, was so neutral, and at that moment I wanted nothing more than to press my fingernails into his eyes. But I spoke calmly. "What is his name now?"

Brano squinted. "This is something that remains between us. You understand?"

"Just tell me his name."

"Ludvík Mas. After he joined the Ministry we gave him a new identity. We didn't want the Czechs to know who he was."

"Ludvík Mas," I said.

"You're not curious why I'm telling you?"

I shook my head. "I don't care. Is he here? Is he in the Capital?"

"He's in Istanbul."

"Istanbul?"

"He left this morning."

"Why?"

"It doesn't matter."

I don't know why I didn't ask more. Sitting there with Brano Sev, my desire for simplicity was acute. Ludvík Mas, or Peter Husák, was in Istanbul. That was all I needed to know. Brano opened his envelope and slid a roll of audiotape to me.

"This is a record of part of my conversation with Peter Husák back in 1968. You may find it of interest."

But all I wanted was simplicity. "I don't need it."

"I think you'll find it useful for understanding."

"Understanding what?"

"The *why* of your boyfriend's death, Katja. And perhaps more. We are sometimes faced with inexplicable moments in our past, and they plague us over the years until we're no longer able to function. But if we find an explanation . . ."

"I didn't think Ministry officers subscribed to psychology, Comrade Sev."

Brano actually smiled. "Not officially, Comrade Drdova. Here."

From the envelope he also took a small bundle of koronas and a fresh maroon passport. An external passport.

"Take this," he said.

On the front page of the passport was an old photograph of me, with my name.

"Comrade Drdova, do you have any travel plans?"

I wasn't sure what to say. At that point I honestly didn't know. "I might."

"Well, if you do, remember that time is of the essence. Also, I'd appreciate it if you'd stay in touch. Give me a call."

"I don't know if I can promise that."

"A call is only a call, Katja. Over a telephone you don't have to say anything you don't wish to say, whereas I can be particularly helpful. I'll be sure to remain near my desk."

"Okay, Brano."

With those words, something moved in me. Though it would soon return, the confusion left, and I felt like a worker receiving instructions that made my entire life a simple matter of obedience.

For that one instant, I felt good.

GAVRA

•

It took a half hour for the Militia technicians to arrive, and Gavra waited for them by the dead American, chain-smoking. Details were accumulating—a hijacked plane, a delusional woman, and the cryptic Ludvík Mas—who, it appeared, killed a German terrorist, a doctor, and an American spy. Now Adrian Martrich was living under the threat of execution.

In the world outside the Ministry, the *why* of these murders wouldn't be of importance. A single man had killed three men in the space of a day and was after a fourth. It didn't matter how the killings were connected to a hijacked plane or to a sick woman who had called from the airport. In the real world, Ludvík Mas would have been picked up and locked in a cell. And Gavra would be allowed to treat him just as he'd treated Wilhelm Adler in that factory office.

But this wasn't the real world. This place was much more elusive, and more threatening.

The men took photographs, carted away the body, and mopped the floor clean.

By the time he returned, Adrian was playing a *Leb i Sol* record and had set two cold vodkas on the coffee table. He smiled at Gavra. "How was your day, dear?"

When the momentary surprise faded, Gavra smiled as well.

They didn't speak at first, only settled into the sofa and sipped their drinks, while over the speakers *Leb i Sol*'s psychedelic jam session settled Gavra's nerves. They toasted their health; then Adrian refilled their glasses and settled next to him on the sofa, close. Gavra said, "Tell me about your sister."

Adrian spoke of a wicked childhood in Chudlove. He described their father's sudden, rabid fits of anger. The two times he broke his son's arm. The day Adrian walked in on him on top of his struggling sister—Zrinka was ten.

Gavra set down his glass.

Adrian told him of the time their father tied their mother to the radiator and made the children watch what he did to her. He told Gavra that she, in turn, focused her frustration on the children. When Father was gone for days on alcoholic rages, Mother blamed them for his disappearances and locked them in the cellar. Then, when Adrian was twelve, they both killed themselves. In the backyard. With knives.

"Did you see the bodies?"

"I watched them do it."

Gavra drank, shaking his head. "Your sister?"

"She was at school."

"No wonder."

"No wonder what?"

"That she believed she had made them kill themselves. She must have dreamed and hoped they would do it. Then, one day, they did."

Adrian gazed at him a moment, then continued. "It was after

that that she became hysterical. The local Militia chief—a fat, useless man—sent her to the Tarabon Clinic. I, on the other hand, lived as a ward of the state in an orphanage outside the Capital, in Zsurk. The less said about that place, the better." He quieted, then said, "I still can't believe she's dead," and laid his head on Gavra's shoulder as Vlatko Stefanovski went into one of his lengthy guitar solos.

Gavra felt his muscles relax beneath Adrian's ear, and when Adrian asked if he would sleep there with him, Gavra took a quick, loud breath and turned to look at the crown of Adrian's head. Adrian raised his face close to Gavra's and kissed him.

Their sex was strange for Gavra, who seldom had affairs inside his own country. He was used to single nights with Turkish boys found at dance clubs, Austrian men picked up from underground bars, and once even an American businessman he met at the airport bar in Frankfurt. During those brief encounters, each participant knew exactly what he wanted; the enjoyment was always visceral. Though in the mornings he was sometimes annoyed or disgusted by his choice the previous night, he never regretted a thing.

With Adrian, the reasons were elusive. Adrian had, in the space of a few days, lost a sister and had his own life threatened. He was looking for comfort. Because of this they acted as if they'd known each other many years. At first they only kissed, and in bed they gripped each other tightly. For the first time in his sexual life, Gavra felt as if he wanted something more than the wonderful violence of sexual organs and wasn't sure why.

Was that love? He didn't know, and it was beside the point—because afterward he passed out, the stress of the last days overcoming him, and slept hard, like a peasant after a long day working the land.

He woke alone in Adrian's bed to the sound of the front door buzzer. The clock told him it was nine, and he could smell coffee.

"Who is it?" he called.

"It's your girlfriend," Adrian said. "Katja's on her way up."

Gavra sprang out of bed, scooped his crumpled clothes in an arm, and swept past Adrian on his way to the bathroom, saying only, "I slept on the couch."

"Good morning to you, too."

While washing himself in the sink and dressing, he heard Katja being let in and offered coffee. Then, in answer to no question at all, Adrian told her, "He's in the bathroom."

Gavra nodded in the mirror. *Okay.* Katja didn't reply, but Adrian felt the need to awkwardly add, "He slept on the couch."

"Oh," said Katja.

Shut up, Adrian.

But Adrian didn't shut up. "Did you hear about the excitement last night?"

Gavra fumbled with the buttons on his shirt, grimacing.

"The dead man was American," Adrian told her. "We don't get many Americans in this neighborhood."

"Dead man?" Katja said as Gavra flung open the door and came out in his socks. Katja, sitting on the couch where Adrian had kissed him, looked up with a confused expression. "Gavra, what the hell happened?"

"There was an incident. I'm going to look into it now."

"Yes? *And?*"

"An American was killed," Adrian added unhelpfully. "You didn't know?"

Gavra glanced at him without kindness and began slipping into his shoes. "Yes, an American. He entered the building and was killed."

"Killed by that man," said Adrian. "What was his name?"

"Not important," said Gavra.

The confusion in Katja's face was shifting into anger. "What do you mean—"

"Later," Gavra said as he reached for his hat. "We'll talk later. See you."

He drove through the morning traffic, trying not to worry about what Adrian might be telling Katja. He'd made a mistake, he knew, sleeping with someone involved with this case—a grieving brother, no less—and felt the unfamiliar queasiness of regret.

The Hotel Metropol was very familiar to him. He'd often come with Brano Sev for meetings in its nondescript rooms, usually to speak with foreign contacts. Gavra knew that in its lobby at any moment were at least three watchers, one of them a young woman well suited to seducing foreign businessmen. The only thing that separated Tania from most prostitutes was that she had a remarkable memory for anything her johns muttered and knew ways to make them mutter almost anything. She was smoking on a padded chair when he entered; she watched him cross directly to the elevator. Gavra spun Timothy Brixton's key on his finger and stepped inside, turning to see Tania rise as the doors slid shut.

Timothy Brixton's room was tidy, cleaned by a maid that morning, with a sheaf of papers on the desk. He went through them, but they were only forms from the Foreign Ministry's Trade Council, requests for trade concessions to bring American televisions into the country. All requests had been denied.

He'd searched a lot of rooms during his apprenticeship, and Brixton's was exceptionally clean. He very much lived his television-salesman cover. Gavra found color brochures for the new twenty-five-inch color set, with young blond women posing as if they came in the box as well.

He rang the front desk and asked for a list of telephone numbers called from this room to be prepared, and when he hung up he noticed the hotel stationery pad. It was clean, but the top page was indented from an earlier note. Using a pencil, he rubbed over it and found the words

Gavra continued through the room, but there was nothing else. So he locked up and showed his Ministry certificate to the desk clerk and asked for the list. While waiting, he noticed that Tania, the hotel's best informer, was no longer around. The clerk handed over a list of five calls, with times and dates beside them. All the numbers were identical, except the last, placed the previous morning at ten, just before Timothy Brixton left the hotel for the last time.

Gavra pointed at the phone on the desk. "May I?"

The clerk shrugged and walked away. Gavra dialed that final number, and after two rings heard a vaguely familiar male voice. "Yes?"

"Uh, who is this?"

The man on the line sounded amused. "Please, Comrade

Noukas. If you don't know who you're calling, then why are you dialing the number?"

Gavra choked a little, and when his voice came out it was a whisper. "Ludvík Mas."

"Hang up now, Gavra."

Gavra did as he was told, and held on to the counter.

An American spy named Timothy Brixton telephoned Ludvík Mas, who gave him the work address for Adrian Martrich. Brixton had no doubt been nearby as Gavra drove Adrian from the butcher shop to his apartment. The American was after Adrian, to learn something, perhaps. But Ludvík Mas had followed the both of them and killed Brixton before he could speak with Adrian.

Amid the confusion, Gavra knew one thing. Adrian Martrich had information of interest to an American spy, and perhaps of interest to Ludvík Mas as well.

There was no doubt: Last night had been a grave mistake. Adrian was hiding something, and his reticence could kill him, or Gavra.

He marched out of the lobby and pushed through the revolving doors, but before he reached his car a short man with a round, flabby face stepped up to him. He had a pistol in his hand.

"Comrade Noukas," he said. "Please come with me."

KATJA

•

Istvan dresses quietly, but I'm awake by the time he's knotting his tie. He gives me a bright morning smile. "Well, hello!"

"Morning," I say with a clotted voice, as if I smoked too many cigarettes the previous night, though I didn't.

"Are you doing the *Sultan Ahmet Camii* today?"

"The what?"

"Blue Mosque," he reminds me, and grins. "I have a feeling you're not one of the world's most fastidious tourists."

I wipe my eyes. "When will you be back?"

"I've got a meeting in an hour, another one at lunchtime, and then another at four." He shrugs. "Six or seven. You'll be here?"

"Of course, Istvan."

After he leaves, there's a knock at the door. I wrap myself in a hotel robe and face a tall man in a uniform holding a box. "Your audio machine, ma'am?"

He places it on the desk and pauses at the door, clearing his throat. Only after he's gone do I realize I was supposed to tip him.

In the Militia we sometimes use these machines, but as I thread the audiotape through the play heads into the take-up reel

I fear I'm doing it wrong, that when I press PLAY the tape will shred and whatever lies on it will remain a mystery. But I'm not as clumsy as I suspect, and soon I'm sitting on the thick carpet in my robe, listening to a tinny conversation through the speaker. Two male voices in a hollow-sounding room. The first voice is plainly Brano Sev's—seven years have changed little with him. The other is a voice I haven't heard for that many years, the slow drawl taking me back to a black month that I have, for years, tried to erase from my daily memories. But here it is again, that voice, and it's telling everything just as I remember it. He makes no excuses. He simply tells the facts as he sees them. He explains that he killed the soldier named Stanislav Klym in order to save himself, that he then moved into Stanislav's apartment and one day opened the door to find Katja Uher, the girlfriend Stanislav had told him about. So he pretended to the girl; he made up stories of his friendship with the boy she loved, saying Stanislav had given him the keys to his apartment and would arrive in another week or so. *She had no reason to doubt it, because this was the kind of guy Stanislav was—he'd give his keys to a stranger just to be hospitable.* At one point he even laughs and says, *I couldn't believe she believed me. Can you believe it?*

People will believe most anything, Comrade Husák.

Two hours later, after listening to it twice through, I pick up the phone and dial.

"This is Sev."

"You're unbelievable."

He lowers his voice. "You're there?"

"It was you. *You.* You knew what he'd done, but you let him stay free. You're a cretin, Brano Sev."

For a moment there's just the hiss of the phone line. "He was useful to us, Comrade Drdova, But now he's served his purpose."

"He's served your purpose."

"Would you like to know where he is?"

"Of course I would."

"The Sultan Inn, in Sultanahmet. On Mustafa Pasa. Number 50."

"Wait." I stumble to the pencil and hotel stationery on the desk, beside the machine. "Repeat that."

He does, and I write it down.

"Are you all right, Comrade Drdova?"

"Oh, me? I'm fine, Comrade Sev. I'm just fantastic." I change tone. "Why are you doing this?"

"What?"

"Helping me find him. I doubt this is in the interests of socialism."

He hums into the telephone, then takes a breath. "This is the final stage in ending something that should have never begun."

"Does this something have to do with Zrinka and Adrian Martrich?"

"Yes."

"With Libarid's death?"

"Everything is connected, Comrade Drdova. And everything I do is in the interests of socialism. Trust me on that."

"No, Brano. Everything you do is in the interests of Brano Sev."

He ignores that. "Are you armed?"

"Armed?"

"I suppose you're not. I want you to do something, but do it right now. It's for your protection. Go to İstiklal Caddesi. It's a street just two blocks from the Hotel Pera Palas, behind the Dutch consulate. Are you writing this down?"

"I am."

"There is a Dutch chapel, the Union Church. Ask for Father Janssen."

"A priest?"

"You'd be surprised where socialism finds its friends, Comrade Drdova. Ask Father Janssen, in these exact words, in English . . . you know English?"

"Not much."

"Just remember this sentence: *Has the harvest come down from the mountains?*"

"What?"

"Those exact words, Comrade Drdova." He repeats the words as I write them. "Father Janssen will give you what you need."

"Brano."

"Yes?"

"How long have you known this? That I was the girl from Peter Husák's story."

"It doesn't matter anymore, Comrade Drdova."

"It does to me."

He pauses. "Your name is different now. You have your husband's name. And it's quite surprising you never ran into each other before, but I suppose Peter Husák didn't come to the Militia offices."

"When?"

"I didn't know until yesterday afternoon at the Metropol, when you told me about your relationship to Stanislav Klym."

Then he hangs up.

For a long time I don't move. I'm standing next to the desk with the buzzing receiver in my hand, and it's all coming back to me. Only once I've replayed it again in my head, that night in all its painful detail, can I put down the phone and go to dress for the day ahead, for what I have to do.

GAVRA

•

His flabby-faced companion drove him out to the Seventh District, to Tolar, a street of low, sooty Habsburg buildings, and parked in front of number 16, behind a white Škoda. He'd taken Gavra's pistol at the hotel, but just inside the front door he returned it. Then he trotted up the stairs; Gavra followed.

The door was on the second floor, and the driver tapped a few times, then waited for the lock to be pulled. Brano Sev opened the door.

"Ah, Gavra. Come in."

The driver remained in the stairwell and pulled the door closed behind them.

It was a sparse office, with empty factory shelves and a single desk. Behind the desk sat Ludvík Mas, his thin mustache, in this light, looking damp. He smiled and motioned to a chair.

Brano was already sitting down.

"Thank you for coming," said Mas. "Comrade Sev felt that you should be made aware of what's going on with your case."

"I'd appreciate that," said Gavra.

"Of course. Brano?"

The colonel turned to him with a straight face. "Gavra, what do you know of parapsychology?"

The question threw him. "Not much. I've heard of Special Department Number 8 in Novosibirsk, but didn't the Russians shut that down?"

"Yes," said Mas. "Six years ago. But research continues."

"The KGB," Brano explained, "controls Soviet research now. But in our country, we set up a laboratory in 1967, in Rokošyn."

Gavra tugged his ear, worried about where this was going. "Zrinka Martrich actually was there?"

Brano shook his head. "Not exactly."

"But she was being experimented on—wasn't she?"

Mas slapped the table and shouted, "Yes!"

Brano chose not to raise his voice. "Comrade Mas is pleased because your supposition is exactly what he hoped others would believe. You see, the research clinic was closed because of lack of results in 1972. The building was torn down. The fact is, there is no research institute anymore."

"Then where was Zrinka Martrich?" Gavra asked. "She's been somewhere for the last three years."

Ludvík Mas said, "She was living her life with us and a few other delusional patients. Elsewhere. What we needed was for her, and the others, to disappear. We plant a few rumors here and there—stories that scientists at Rokošyn have made sudden breakthroughs—and the story is complete. Zrinka Martrich, the rumors go, is at the center of a project to tame the forces of psychokinesis and use them to stomp out the Western imperialists. Beautiful!"

Gavra looked from one face to the other. "I don't understand."

Brano leaned forward, slipping into the familiar tone of the educator. "It's a Ministry counterintelligence project. We plant evidence of a nonexistent psychokinetic project in order to lure Western spies into the country. The Ministry controls the flow of information to these foreign agents. The spies can then be identified by this method, tracked, and interrogated."

"Or liquidated," said Mas, his chin settling on his chest. "I've been very pleased by the results. In the last two years we've taken care of two British, a French, and two American agents—poor Mr. Brixton included." Mas raised his eyebrows. "Brixton even made it as far as Rokošyn—just to be more puzzled when he found no clinic. But that didn't stop him searching. You saw the fruits of our labor in Adrian Martrich's stairwell."

"*Smert shpionam,*" said Gavra.

"Death to spies," said Mas.

Gavra turned to Brano. "Are you telling me that the plane was part of this? You killed sixty-eight passengers as part of a *hoax?*"

Mas shook his head. "Now *that* is something we had nothing to do with. We put Comrade Martrich on the plane to Istanbul, yes. We wanted to try the same ruse in Turkey—our embassy is riddled with leaks, and by having her there, by placing a few rumors, we thought we could clean the place out." He grunted. "The fucking Armenians we never predicted."

"Like I told you before, Gavra," said Brano, "it was a coincidence."

Mas lit a cigarette. "A tragic coincidence. Tragic in the obvious way, but now the Comrade Lieutenant General is closing down the operation. Zrinka Martrich was our central character in the scheme, and with her dead the operation is losing its momentum. We've had a good run, but now it's over."

"Which is why," said Brano, "we've had these deaths."

"We're cleaning up the loose ends," said Mas.

"Because they're connected to the operation," Gavra said, not sure anymore what to believe. "But what about Wilhelm Adler? You called him—you told him about the plane."

"Not me." Mas raised his hands. "Adler wasn't part of the operation. But if he was working with these terrorists, he didn't deserve to live. As for Doctor Arendt, he simply knew too much. He would begin to ask questions about his old patient."

"What about the others?" said Gavra. "The other patients."

Mas shrugged, clearly unwilling to answer. "The reason you're being told all of this is that I need you to do two things."

Gavra settled back into his chair, arms crossed over his chest.

"First, I need silence. In particular, you are not to breathe a word of this to your partner, that—what's her name?"

"Comrade Drdova," Brano told him.

"Yes," said Mas. "Is that understood?"

Gavra nodded.

"Second, I want you to remain with Adrian Martrich. I'm waiting to find out what we'll do with him. It's possible the Comrade Lieutenant General will want to use that faggot in another way."

Gavra opened his mouth but didn't speak.

Mas winked—a secret communication. "Yes, comrade. He's got the capitalist disease. Just watch out for yourself when you're with him."

"What if he isn't of use?" Gavra asked.

Mas looked at Brano, who spoke quietly and, Gavra believed, reluctantly. "Then you'll be asked to kill him, Comrade Noukas."

Gavra eased his hand down because it had jumped to his ear.

KATJA

•

On a rack in the lobby of the Pera Palas I find a tourist map that I study just outside the front door, in the hot light. Hotels and restaurants are marked by childish hand-drawn icons of roofs. At the bottom, beyond the Galata Bridge that crosses the Golden Horn where it flows from the Bosphorus, and through a tangle of ancient streets, is a comical roof marked SULTAN INN, a block north of the Sea of Marmara, which they call *Marmara Denizi*.

This is my first time outside, under the Turkish sun. A line of dirty cars pushes by, and pedestrians wander in all directions. In other circumstances, I would be thrilled just to stand here.

As Brano told me, the Union Church is only two blocks away, straight from the hotel, up an alley, across İstiklal Caddesi, full of overpriced shops and multilingual tourists, then down another alley to where a small sign points me to a door in an ancient wall. As it also houses the Dutch consulate, a guard asks my nationality. I tell him and ask for the church. With a smile, he points me up a cobbled path inside.

It's a small, modest place, in some ways similar to the Catholic chapel in Pácin, where I grew up. Since moving to the Capital years ago, I've found myself reluctant to return to see my family. Perhaps it's just an aspect of growing up, but when I do return and walk with Mother arm in arm past that chapel, I always feel as if I'm visiting another country. I told this once to Aron, but he didn't understand. He snorted under his breath, pulled up his sheet, and turned off the bedroom light.

The inner walls of the Union Church are rough, striped by slender bricks, and only two people sit in the pews, far from each other. I spot an old man dusting the pulpit with a feathered brush. He looks up when I approach.

"*Evet?*"

"Father Janssen," I say.

He frowns, then speaks in labored English. "I do not know Janssen, a father."

My English is just as labored. "Is priest here?"

He considers this, and it's one of those moments when I'm pleased to be a woman because I present no threat. "Come," he says, and leads me back to the front. Above our heads, over the entrance, is a second floor filled with an old pipe organ. The cleaner leads me upstairs to the dim floor, where a black-suited priest is reading a book laid on the organ keys. He looks up. "*Evet?*"

The cleaner says a few words in Dutch that I can't make out, though I can tell that this priest's name is Van der Berg. Then the cleaner says, "Janssen," and the priest's eyes light up. He nods for the old man to leave as he smiles at me. He doesn't speak until the cleaner is visible again over the railing, headed for the altar.

"What can I do for you, ma'am?"

I close my eyes, trying to remember. "Is the harvest come down on the mountains?"

Van der Berg bites his lip, then lowers his voice and speaks in my language. "It has indeed, my child. A moment."

Beneath a stained-glass window is a low bookshelf filled with twenty leather-bound books. He peers back down the length of the chapel, then pulls out a book called *Sygdommen til Døden* and opens it.

Just like in the movies, I think.

It's a hollowed-out book, containing a silk-wrapped package that he hands to me. I unwrap it and look at the small Turkish MKE pistol, .380 caliber, not unlike the Walther PPs I used for practice in the Militia Academy.

"There are seven," he whispers, tapping the handle. "Will you need more?"

"What?"

"Cartridges. Do you need more than seven?"

I shake my head.

He holds out his hand. "Please. The scarf."

I give him the silk scarf and put the gun into my handbag.

"Is there anything else?"

I hesitate, looking into his kindly face, trying to think. Maybe some direction, that's something I could use, but that's not why he's here.

He smiles. "You're new to this, aren't you?"

I blink.

"Just remember, maintain your calm. And afterward, get rid of it."

"Here?"

"No, silly girl. The Bosphorus. I don't know how many guns that waterway has swallowed."

"I see."

The priest glances back again at the empty pews, then says in a high whisper, "For the victory of the world's proletariat!"

"Of course," I mutter, then turn to go.

The map helps. It takes me up İstiklal Caddesi to an underground train, the Tünel, which brings me down to the Galata Bridge. I cross on foot. Men line the railing clutching fishing poles. Then I'm making my way through hot, narrow streets, ignoring voices—*Hello pretty lady*; *Sprechen Sie Deutsch?* Finally, I reach Mustafa Pasa, a busy avenue choked with shops selling bronze sculptures and carpets and food.

The Sultan Inn is unassuming and run-down, not the kind of place I expect to find an officer of the Ministry for State Security. Or maybe I'm just inexperienced (which I am) and naive (which I may be). The lobby is dark, not made for the world's tourists, but the bald desk clerk in the sweat-stained undershirt is smiling broadly at me. "Heh-*low,*" he says.

I've already made a mistake. Walking inside only announces my presence. So I give him a confused expression and step backward across the cracked tiles. "Sorry. Wrong address."

He shrugs as if it's an opportunity missed.

Across the street I buy coffee from a street vendor and sip it beside a carpet shop. Passersby bump into me, and the occasional beggar demands things with open hands. It's five o'clock, and the low-lying sun at the end of the street makes me flush.

"Madam," says a shriveled old man. "You are lost?"

I shake my head and turn away.

"Can I be of assistance, perhaps? Show you Istanbul?"

I give him my Militia stare. The one where you momentarily

separate from your body and display the full force of your scorn. "Leave me alone."

It works as well here as it does back home—the old man moves on—but the Militia stare is only a façade. I'm having trouble focusing on the faces in the street. What would Aron do now? We've traveled together to Krakow and the Black Sea, and he knows how to take care of me when I stumble like this.

He would put his arm around my shoulders and guide me to a café where the time could settle down again. Blurred faces surge toward me, and I know that if Peter Husák comes I won't even see him.

I step into the carpet shop to catch my breath, but suddenly two salesmen are on me. "The lovely madam, so very proud we are that such a lovely madam is interested in our carpets!"

I rub my face. "No."

"Original Turkish, handwoven. Touch!"

"A taxi," I say. "Please. Just call a taxi for me."

GAVRA

•

Brano drove him back to the Metropol to retrieve his car. They rode in silence until Gavra cleared his throat. "There's something wrong with this."

"I know," said Brano. "There's a lot wrong with this."

"Then what are you doing about it?"

Brano turned up Yalta Boulevard. "It's best you're kept in the dark, Gavra. I know you don't like this, and despite what you may believe, I don't enjoy keeping things from you. But I am working on it."

"Tell me about Ludvík Mas."

Brano took a breath. "He used to be like you, Gavra. Some years ago I brought him into the Ministry. He was young, intelligent, and eager to please. But he was also desperate for power. I didn't see that; it's my fault. Once I realized my error, it was too late. He had gone over my head—and against my orders—when he set up Room 305. This office began with the operation you've just heard about, a fraud around parapsychology, but has since expanded considerably. The Lieutenant General calls it 'Disruption Services,' because its various operations also work to disrupt capitalist countries' internal workings. Often by funding dissident groups."

"Like terrorists."

Brano nodded. "Once Ludvík had set it up, under the protection of the Lieutenant General, I could do nothing to stop him."

"So you disagree with the operation."

"Like I said, I told him not to begin it. It's always been my belief that the Ministry should not be involved in the haphazard murder of foreign agents. But others above me felt differently."

He parked behind Gavra's car and turned off the engine, then stared out the windshield at the opaque windows of the Hotel Metropol. "Gavra," he said, "I want you to be very careful. I don't trust that Mas won't try something again, and you'll be in danger. He knows as well as I do that you're a homosexual, and for that reason he places little value on your life. He's that kind of person."

Gavra felt as if his chest were being squeezed. His vision was fuzzy. "You know?"

Brano surprised him by patting his knee. "Of course I know. And I knew that was no girl in your bed back in Istanbul. My only concern is that you keep such things quiet. You can't afford to be . . ." He paused, as if the next word were not part of his vocabulary: "Flamboyant. It could ruin your career. Or worse."

Gavra was at first unable to think of a reply, but then it occurred to him. "Thank you, Comrade Sev."

Brano placed his hands on the wheel again. "It's nothing, Gavra. Though I do suggest you avoid becoming involved with Adrian Martrich."

"Of course."

"But watch him. Make sure Katja stays away. This doesn't need to spread any further than it already has."

"Yes, comrade." Gavra opened the door and climbed into the hot sunlight.

He returned to find Katja and Adrian in the living room, drinking cans of Zipfer beer. Katja was in a state. She was pulling at her hair, making it dirty, and when she noticed Gavra she spoke with an unfocused voice. "Okay, you can tell me now."

"What?" Gavra asked as innocently as he could manage.

She pointed at him. "Everything."

Adrian shrugged at his questioning glance.

She said, "I don't appreciate being left in the dark. You've been meeting with a man named Peter Husák, correct?"

"I don't know who that is," said Gavra.

Katja stood, the beer in her hand. "Either you tell me what's going on, or I'm walking out of here right now, and you can take care of this yourself."

Perhaps it was Brano Sev's half-remembered training coming back, but Gavra became hard at that moment. His jaw tensed, squaring his face. He said, "I can't tell you. If you want to leave, then fine."

Katja walked over to him and emptied the rest of her beer on his shirt. Before leaving, she said, "Sorry about the floor, Adrian."

"No problem," said Adrian.

PETER

•

Seven years later, with a new life, a family, a position and a new name, Peter sat at an outdoor café table between the Blue Mosque and Aya Sofia, on Mimar Mehmet Ağa Caddesi. He did not like Istanbul. It was unbearably hot, packed with the unwashed wretches of Islam, and the noise—what they generously called "music"—was inescapable. Even the mornings were filled with mournful muezzins who climbed their minarets and moaned wobbly prayers for the whole city to suffer through. And this was the city where, eight days ago, he'd stood in the airport waiting for a plane that would never arrive, wondering if its absence marked the end of his career.

He'd arrived badly, of course. A rough flight followed by a swarthy taxi driver who charged him three times the going rate to get to the Sultan Inn, then a hot room that opened onto the noise and stink of Mustafa Pasa, allowing him no sleep.

But his career had not ended—not yet—because he'd recovered swiftly, explaining to the Comrade Lieutenant General that the entire Rokošyn operation would be cleaned up, and soon. That was why he was here. It would be as if the operation had never existed, and the other departments of Disruption Services could continue unabated.

And the old man, always a sucker for easy solutions, only told him, *Just clean it up fast.* Had the Lieutenant General known what he knew about Zrinka Martrich, and how the Armenians ended up on *her* plane, he would have said something entirely different.

Up the street, a *tablah*-and-*buzuq* street duo made terrible sounds, and Peter felt again that all this could be dealt with, were it not for the music. That incessant, moronic percussion and those tinny, agonizing strings doing their best to remain out of tune. All in praise of fat, coin-adorned belly dancers.

The sweating man at the table with him—another fat one—no doubt loved all the chaos. That music was made for him. Like the music, this Turk lacked any trace of subtlety. After shaking Peter's hand, he patted the table and spoke in his heavily accented English. "So you have it? The money?"

Peter admitted that he did have the money.

"I can see?"

Peter placed his elbows on the table. Beyond the shade of the café's umbrellas, the unwashed throbbed, sometimes spilling in, grimy children bumping into the backs of chairs. "Not until I have my information," said Peter.

The fat Turk frowned, then sipped his tea. He was a captain in their police force, used sometimes by this or that side of the Great

Game for a nugget of information. It was perhaps the only trait that Peter shared with Captain Talip Evren: Neither had ever known the conviction of the zealot. Evren pursed his damp lips. "You like Istanbul, Comrade . . . ?"

"I love it, Captain. And the music . . . what a people." When he said this he made no expression to suggest he meant it.

Captain Evren grinned. "It is a sin . . . sin*cere* place, comrade. We are very open people. Sometime, sometime foreigners, they think we are very foolish. Stupid even. But you know in Ottoman time we are making algebra when you make fire with sticks."

Peter leaned forward. "I don't care what you were doing a thousand years ago. What I care about, Captain, is the reason I'm carrying two hundred Deutschmarks in my pocket right now."

"You're in the hurry, comrade! Why not a cup of tea?"

Peter hushed the shout before it reached his throat. Maybe it wasn't the noise or the stink or the heat soaking his thin shirt that got to him; maybe it was simply that in Istanbul, the scene of his most complete failure, he so easily lost control of himself.

He took a breath.

He lit a cigarette.

"No, thank you, Captain. I'm not thirsty."

The captain pointed at the cigarette pack on the table. "May I?"

Peter tapped one out, handed it over, and lit it for him.

Behind a cloud of smoke, the captain said, "You ask for this man."

"That's right."

"According to the border record, this Adrian Martrich, he is on our Turkish soil."

"Okay, then," said Peter. "The hotel."

The Turk scratched his cheek. "Well, this is not so . . ."

"Two hundred Deutschmarks," said Peter. "Not a schilling more. So stop wasting my time."

Captain Evren allowed himself a brief, admiring smile. "The Hotel Erboy, in the Sirkeci neighborhood. Ebusuud Caddesi, number 32. Check in two nights ago. Not by himself."

"I know. What room?"

"Three-oh-five."

Peter hesitated, never trusting coincidences. "Three hundred and five."

"Yes."

"And there's no doubt about this?"

The captain shook his head. "The registration, it come yesterday. Of course, it is always possible he will have change hotel, but this very morning I call the Erboy. Is there still." He put out the unfinished cigarette. "These are very rough for my pink lungs. You have the money?"

On his walk north toward the Golden Horn, crushed by the heat of all those bodies, he wished, as he often did, for his farmhouse. He wished for his wife, Ilza, and four-year-old Iulian, but most of all he wished for that house with its magnificent expanse of empty, rolling fields outside Baia Mare. No one in sight. It was ten in the morning, and at this moment Ilza would have driven Iulian to the village school—the only student in the village to be brought by car—and she would now be in the market, picking over vegetables still dirty from the fields. His wife was accustomed to his long absences—they both were—and she recognized that because of his absences they lived better than anyone they knew. She complained sometimes, of course, because life in the provinces could get to you, leave you longing for the kinetic life of the Capital. But he had explained it enough times. Their home was a refuge from the world. He knew more of the world than his provincial wife did, and she had to trust him when he told her that it was an unimaginably cruel and forbidding place.

He crossed the Galata Bridge lined with fishermen, rode the Tünel up the hill, and continued north to the small Union Church at the Dutch consulate. The inside was peaceful, clean like only the Dutch could pull off in this dirty city, with dark wood pews leading to a small altar. Ilza would have liked this. She was always taken in by the solemnity of religious cults. One lone tourist shared the chapel with him, a young woman reading a guidebook in a pew, no doubt escaping the heat. He ignored her and took the stairs up to the balcony, which held the chapel's pipe organ.

Father Janssen, whose real name was something entirely different, was eating an egg sandwich at the organ's stool. He looked like he didn't appreciate the interruption of his lunch.

"*Evet?*"

Peter glanced around, but they were alone. He said in clear English, "Are you Father Janssen?"

The priest squinted and laid down his sandwich. "Again?"

"Again what?"

"I am called Father Janssen."

"Has the harvest come down from the mountains?"

Father Janssen shook his head. "This isn't an armory, you know."

"Of course. I just know that—"

"Your people already have it."

"What do you mean?"

"Just what I said. Someone came this morning and picked it up. I haven't had time to replace it."

"Who?"

"How should I know? I don't even know who you are." He wagged a finger at Peter. "And I don't want to know."

It was simple bad luck. Poor timing. As he made his way south again, back across the Galata toward his hotel, he almost found it amusing that even such a straightforward cleanup operation could always, in a city like this, unravel.

He could still get hold of a pistol, but it would take time. He could walk to the *Kapali Çarsisi* and search for the men who floated on the edge of the Grand Bazaar's teeming crowds, their eyes attuned to extravagant tourists and undercover policemen. He'd find one who looked willing, then explain his need. A meeting would be arranged, somewhere discreet, and terms would be established. The price—that would require an hour of hateful but obligatory haggling. Then, and only then, would a final meeting be arranged. But by that point it would probably be too late; the queer would have made his way to another city.

At least he'd had the foresight to bring along the old hunting

knife he'd acquired seven years ago. He'd brought it for sentimental reasons, as he always did when leaving the country for work,
but never thought that he'd have to depend on it to kill Adrian
Martrich.

KATJA

•

I didn't plan it. Not really. It was something that had to be done. I needed an escape, and this man, this soldier—he was the opportunity. Do you know what I mean? This guy, you see, he had everything. He had an apartment and a girl he was going to marry. He had a life. What did I have? I didn't have a thing. Do you think that's fair? Do you think I was any less brave than him? I told you what I did, what I did to my own friends. Did Stanislav ever have the courage or the presence of mind to do what I did? No, because he never had to. This is what I couldn't accept. Because of circumstances beyond our control, he was someone, and I was not. So I took that drunk bastard out of that bar, I went with him to the Charles Bridge, and I stabbed him. I took his papers, his keys, and his money.

Don't think I enjoyed it. I was only doing what was necessary. But at the same time I didn't shy from it. I can admit to some confusion, yes. And at the border I was not as composed as I would have liked. But the border guards didn't notice, nor did they stare too closely at the photo in his passport. That's the funny thing. It wasn't me in that picture, but they didn't even realize. And I understood then that there

*are more things possible in this world than we realize. With a straight
face and a bit of courage you can do anything.*

I dial with shaking fingers and listen to the monotone ring. Then
he answers.

"Aron?"

"Katja? Is that you? Where the hell are you? I've been—"

"I'm not in town. I just . . . how are you?"

"What do you mean, how am I? I've been worried sick. No one
in the Militia knows where you are, and that chief of yours, Emil,
he called asking if you were at home—where *are* you?"

"Listen, Aron, I can't tell you about it now. But I'm okay. I'm
fine."

"You're having an affair, aren't you?"

"What?"

"That Ministry guy you always talk about. Gavra. He's gone
missing, too. I'm not a fool."

That gives me pause, because I can't imagine how he could
suspect such a thing—where is this coming from? I say, "Sometimes you are a fool, Aron," but really, he's not. Not at all. Had
Gavra ever given me the slightest sign, I would have slept with
him without a second thought.

He tries to think through his words. "I know we have our
problems, Kati. Hell, we have more than most. But this isn't the
way to deal with them."

"I'm not having an affair."

"Whatever you want to call it, I don't care. Just come home,
okay? We'll work it out."

I even smile to myself then. Aron is wonderful at deluding
himself and making things sound so easy. We've been trying for

three years to work out our problems, and it's the hardest thing in the world. "I just wanted you to know I was all right."

"Come home, Katja."

Despite the smile, I'm choking up. He can hear the soft sound that always precedes my tears, and it gives him hope. He thinks it's a sign I'm weakening. But he's never been able to read me because I've never taught him how.

"It's not a problem, Kati. Really. You come home and we'll talk. We'll take a vacation together. I'll talk to my supervisor and arrange time off. But you have to come home first."

Aron will never understand. So I say, "I'll see you in a few days. Okay?"

"Now."

"A few days." Then, almost as an afterthought: "And I love you."

"Christ, Kati."

I hang up and get off the bed and walk past the tape player out to the terrace, where the sun has set over minarets and domes and decomposing Ottoman rooftops. A hot, stinky breeze rises from the street, bringing with it the choked sound of automobiles and shouting vendors. I'm shaking. Maybe that's only because I haven't eaten a thing all day.

The telephone rings. I look at it from the terrace for a while before coming back inside to get it.

"Hello?"

"Katja, it's me."

"How did you get this number? I didn't tell you where I was."

"It doesn't matter, Katja. Did you see him today?"

"Not yet."

"Just know that he's changed hotels. He's now in the Erboy.

Ebusuud Caddesi, number 32. Under the name Ryzsard Knopek. Room 512."

"And how do you know this?"

"Because he reported in, Comrade Drdova."

"I see."

Brano Sev hangs up.

GAVRA

•

Once Katja had slammed the door on her way out, Adrian gave him a kiss on the cheek, took his beer-stained shirt from him, and soaked it in the bathroom sink. Gavra poured vodkas in the kitchen and brought them to the bathroom, where he sat on the toilet.

"Not going to tell me either?" said Adrian, as he squeezed the shirt and plunged it back in the water.

Gavra downed his vodka. "I'm sorry."

"State secrets and all that?"

"And all that." He left to refill his glass.

In the kitchen, Gavra wondered again why he did this job. Unlike Brano Sev, he was a man without belief—in the promise of socialism, or even the maintenance of world peace. And no matter what he believed, the job was never about such grandiose ideals. It was always like this, like standing in an apartment waiting for a phone call asking you to kill a man you've made love to. While he'd never before been asked to do this particular thing, it wasn't so different from the lies he'd been asked to hand out to enemies of the state, the gradual confidence tricks he'd used to ensnare political opponents—tasks that often left him with a hole in his stomach that could only be filled by shots of hard liquor.

He had nothing else; that was true. He'd ostracized his family long ago and given himself up to the strange solitude of the Ministry for State Security, which had become the only world he knew. But was this reason enough to stay?

Adrian laid the wet shirt on the radiator and placed his empty glass on the kitchen table for Gavra to refill. Then he pulled up a chair and sat with his legs crossed at the knee.

"You've been lying to me," said Gavra.

"Have I?"

"You know more than you've let on, and it's going to have to end. Now."

Adrian looked into his glass, rotating it with his fingertips. "She called me."

"Who? Zrinka?"

He nodded but didn't speak. When he sniffed, Gavra understood.

"She called you from the airport."

"Yes," he said. "She called to say good-bye. And to give me instructions. To tell me things she said I didn't need to understand but should only do." He looked up at Gavra. "I trust my sister. My sister was a saint."

"Tell me what she said."

"Can I have another?"

Gavra refilled his glass.

He sipped. "She knew she wouldn't survive that plane ride, and she knew what would follow. She said that I would meet a man— you—and that we would become very close. She even used the word 'love.' "

Gavra waited.

"She told me that I should do two things, and she told me when to do them. Exactly when."

"To do what?"

"The first thing I've done. I did it a few hours ago. I took Katja to where you went today. Tolar Street, number 16."

Gavra pressed his forehead with a palm. "*What?*"

"I don't know why. She told me to take Katja there at precisely three o'clock on Monday the twenty-eighth of April, and wait. Just wait. So I did. Katja didn't want to go, but I told her it was important—important for her to understand things. We went and sat in the car. I didn't know what to expect. And then the door opened and you left with Brano Sev. He drove you somewhere. That surprised her, but she still didn't understand. She asked me again why we were there, but I didn't know what to say. Then the door opened again, and we saw a small, tough-looking guy come out, followed by another man. He had a very thin mustache. That was it. You should have seen her face. It was—it was unbelievable. She almost wept. We watched them drive off. Then I brought her back here. That's why she was so upset when you wouldn't tell her anything. That's why she got you wet."

The light in the apartment was failing, and Gavra had trouble seeing Adrian's face clearly. "Your sister," he said. "She *told* you this?"

"Yes," he said. "She has a knack for knowing things."

"Had."

Adrian nodded. "Had."

"How did she know Katja? Or me? Did she meet us?"

"No," said Adrian. "She just knew."

"I don't believe it."

He shrugged. "I'm not asking you to believe anything, Gavra. I'm just telling you what happened."

"What's the second thing?"

"What second thing?"

"The second thing she asked you to do."

"What time is it?"

Gavra checked his watch. "Quarter after six."

Adrian frowned, considering this. "It's not time yet."

"Tell me."

"Okay," said Adrian. "But don't go doing anything. Just wait. Can you promise me that?"

"I can't promise you anything."

Adrian looked at Gavra's shoes, which were dirty. "At eight, you're going to get a call here. From Brano Sev. Wait for him to call. He will. When he calls, tell him that the hijackers were not a surprise. Not to Zrinka, and not to Ludvík Mas. And it was no coincidence that he put her on that particular plane. It was a test."

"I don't understand."

"You don't have to understand, dear. The message is for Brano Sev, not you."

"I should call him now."

"No," said Adrian. "That's not how she planned it."

Gavra rubbed his eyes. He could hardly see a thing. "This doesn't make any *sense.* How could she know these things?"

"I told you, Gavra. She had a knack for knowing things. She always did, even when she was a child."

"So she wasn't delusional?"

"Of course not. Unlike most saints, my sister was never delusional."

"I need to think about this."

"Go ahead. Lie in bed, and I'll cook us something to eat."

Gavra wasn't sure what to do. Ludvík Mas's story of a complex ruse to snare foreign agents played and replayed in his head. Was it possible that the real ruse was Zrinka Martrich herself—that she was, in fact, the real thing? Doctor Arendt had talked of "thought broadcasting," the ability to influence other people's actions, which was plainly impossible. Yet even the Russians had invested millions of rubles into such research. If it were true, then was Zrinka put through a test to stop a group of Armenian terrorists from hijacking a plane?

"If she had some kind of . . . *powers* . . . then why didn't she stop the terrorists?"

Adrian stood up. "I don't know. She told me she wouldn't survive the flight. Maybe she didn't want to survive it. Come on," he said, rubbing Gavra's shoulders. "Take a rest."

Despite himself, Gavra did what Adrian asked. He took off his dirty shoes and climbed into Adrian's bed, blinking in the darkness. He could hear his host going through pots and pans, the puff of the stove being lit, the refrigerator opening and closing.

He remembered what Ludvík Mas had said to someone on the telephone in Atatürk International: *It does appear she didn't play along.* Then the urgent, confused voice of the Armenian hijacker: *She said it. She's one of yours. Yes. Because she knows even more. She told me. How did she know?*

He sat up and rubbed his face again just as the telephone in the other room rang. The clock beside the bed said seven thirty.

Adrian's surprised voice drifted back to him: "He's *early*."

Gavra went into the living room and approached the phone. Adrian was cooking chicken breast in a pan. "Go ahead. It's for you."

On the seventh ring, Gavra picked it up.

"Hello."

"Gavra," said Brano. "I thought I should be the one to call, rather than Mas."

"Yes?"

"I'm afraid the order has come down from the Comrade Lieutenant General. About Adrian Martrich. You are going to have to do it."

"Oh."

"Listen, it doesn't have to be you. I'll come over and take care of it myself. I know how hard it can be, particularly when you've spent so much time with the subject."

Gavra blinked toward the kitchen, where Adrian whistled as he cooked. The *subject*. Ministry terminology drove him crazy. "I have a message for you," he said.

"What?"

"It's originally from Zrinka Martrich, before she died."

"A letter?"

"No," said Gavra. "She called her brother from the airport and asked him to pass a message on to you."

"Me?" Brano paused. "She used my name?"

"Apparently so."

"But I never met—"

"She seemed to know a lot of people she never met. I can't explain it."

He could hear Brano Sev breathing. "What's the message?"

"That Ludvík Mas knew about the hijacking before it happened. And that's why Zrinka was on that plane. It was a test."

"A test? What kind of test?"

Gavra bit his lip. He didn't know how to say this. "It seems that what Ludvík Mas told us was only partly true. The research was real, and Zrinka Martrich was . . . She had abilities that they wanted to use."

Brano didn't speak for a moment. Gavra waited for him to say that this changed everything, that there was no need for him to kill Adrian Martrich. But Brano only said, "Thank you for the message."

"And?"

"And what?"

"What you asked me to do."

Brano's breaths were very heavy as he considered this. "I'm afraid that doesn't change. The order comes from the Lieutenant General, who no doubt knows everything already."

"But—"

"Do you want me to come over?"

"No, comrade," said Gavra. "I'll take care of it."

It was possible that he knew what he'd do while he was speaking to Brano, but more likely, he didn't know until afterward as they sat over plates of chicken and fried potatoes in silence. Adrian didn't ask a thing, only ate quietly, waiting for Gavra to say something. Finally he did.

"Adrian, I want you to pack a suitcase and get your passport." He paused, reconsidering. "Do you *have* an external passport?"

"Of course," said Adrian. "She asked me that as well."

PETER

•

His walk north from the Sultan Inn was long and overly strenuous, his suitcase catching knees and earning him quick, dark looks. So, despite his desire for anonymity, he flagged a taxi at a crowded intersection and settled into the hot backseat.

"*Alo,*" said the driver.

"The Hotel Erboy."

Peter had been in the Ministry since 1968, brought in by the moderately legendary Colonel Brano Oleksy Sev. Stories went around about the peculiar small man who usually chose not to speak but instead leveled his piercing gaze on you until the nervousness shook you to pieces. Colonel Sev had arrived at the apartment and mistaken him for the other man—*Comrade Private Stanislav Klym?* In his shock, Peter had said, *Yes?*

After that first week of security interrogations and the final uncovering of his true identity, Peter—now Ludvík Mas—spent a year training in those barracks outside Dibrivka, the "secret school" where the techniques of intelligence and subterfuge were reduced to dry lesson plans.

He left the school fit and clearheaded and bursting with the

desire to please, so he worked hard for two years at the menial intelligence jobs handed out to the lower ranks. Pick up this man.
Camp out in this room and keep the audiotape recording. Take
this package to there. Destroy these documents.

He'd followed his orders well up until December 1971. In the
Ministry headquarters on Yalta Boulevard he'd taken a bulky file
downstairs to the incinerator, but on the way stepped into a bathroom. He closed himself into a stall and began to read.

Why should he not share in the state's secrets?

The file began with an overview of the history of the USSR's
studies into "psychotronics," beginning with Bernard Bernar-
dovich Kazhinsky's Tblisi experiments into telepathy, which led,
in 1922, to an address on "human thought-electricity" to the All-
Russian Congress of the Association of Naturalists. Later, Leonid
L. Vasiliev took up the mantle, focusing on the use of mental sug-
gestion in his 1962 book, *Biological Radio Communication.* And
in 1966, sixty Russian researchers were brought to Academ-
gorodok, or Science City, on the Ob River in western Siberia, to
work in the Institute of Automation and Electrometry's Special
Department Number 8. Because of a lack of results, the entire department was closed in 1969.

This historical summary had been used to justify the continued
use of the research institute in Rokošyn. Since 1967, scientists there
had been attempting to harness "psi particles," which could poten-
tially allow global communication among special Ministry officers,
without the need of hazardous radio transmitters.

But the Rokošyn project, the final document told him, was being scrapped.

As Peter slipped the pages into the incinerator's fire, a plan was
already forming.

The Hotel Erboy was filled with American tourists sagging on padded chairs and fanning themselves with wrinkled maps. Like its façade, the lobby was modern, with wood paneling and inset lamps above the front desk. Peter handed his passport to an amiable clerk. "A room, please."

"Of course" said the clerk in English, looking at the document. "Mister *Ree*-zahrd Knopek."

"Ryzsard Knopek."

"Of course," said the clerk, making a note of this. "And you will find breakfast downstairs in our Paşazade Restaurant from seven until ten thirty in the morning. Free, of course, of charge."

In his narrow room, he waited for the international operator to connect him. It took a while, but finally a woman's voice said, "Importation Register, First District."

"Hello, Regina. This is Ludvík. Is the Comrade Lieutenant General available?"

"Just a moment," she said coolly. Regina Haliniak, at the Yalta front desk, had never liked him.

The line clicked, then buzzed twice before he heard the Lieutenant General's booming greeting. "Ludvík, you old bastard! How's the weather down there?"

"Hot, comrade."

"Do you have good news for me?"

"Everything will be cleaned up by tomorrow afternoon."

"Excellent, Ludvík. I knew I could depend on you."

Peter nodded self-consciously into the receiver, as if the Lieutenant General were there to see. "I only had a question."

"Shoot."

"Has someone else arrived here in the last day or so?"

"Besides the obvious pair, you mean?"

"Exactly."

The Lieutenant General paused, humming. "Not that I know of. Brano!"

Through the hiss of the line he heard Brano Sev's weak voice in the Lieutenant General's office. *Yes?*

"Comrade Sev's there with you?"

"Did you want to speak with him?"

"No."

The Lieutenant General's voice lowered as he asked Brano Sev if he knew of any new operatives in Istanbul. "He's shaking his head, Ludvík. Comrade Sev's a man of few words."

"Yes. I know."

He could hear the Lieutenant General's *uh huh, uh huh* in answer to something Brano was saying. Then: "We'll double-check here and get back to you if we learn something. Where will you be?"

"The Hotel Erboy," said Peter. "It's where the others are."

"You'll be under Knopek again?"

"Yes, comrade."

Peter hung up and stretched out on the bed, closing his eyes. While he trusted the Lieutenant General, he didn't like the fact that his original mentor, Brano Sev, was there. He and Brano were not enemies, per se, but nor were they friends at this point. Friends often grow apart over the space of weeks or months for a variety of reasons; yet with Brano he knew the exact day and hour, the precise reason.

18 April 1972. One o'clock.

At Peter's request, they met at their usual bench in Victory Park, beside the statue to the dead of all wars, the bronze soldier on a boulder, his rifle lying across his knees. Peter said he had an idea.

"So Comrade Junior Lieutenant Mas has an idea."

Peter ignored the tone. "A method for uncovering imperialist spies."

"Go on."

"Well, the Russians had Special Department Number 8, and we had the Rokošyn clinic. To study the potential use of psychokinesis. It was recently closed down."

Brano Sev looked at him. "I hope you're not suggesting we use mystics to give us the names of enemy agents."

"Not at all, Comrade Colonel. What I'm suggesting is that we reopen the Rokošyn project, which will, ostensibly, continue investigating paranormal phenomena."

"Why?"

"Bear with me, Comrade Colonel. Please."

Brano Sev folded his hands in his lap.

"On paper, the clinic would keep up the pretense of this work. Our mental homes are full of people who believe they have special abilities, and they would be brought to that remote mountain facility."

"To be studied?"

"No, Comrade Colonel. They would simply be cared for in the same manner they're cared for now. No actual research would be conducted."

"You realize," said Brano Sev, "that you're making less and less sense as you continue."

"This is where my reasoning lies: The program would be given the highest level of security clearance."

"Yes?"

"However, we would sometimes allow pieces of information to slip out—about a major parapsychology program that's achieving great success. This, in turn, will pique the interests of the imperialists. They will mobilize their embedded agents, and perhaps send new ones. But because we control the outflow of information, we will be able to identify and track foreign agents in our midst."

Peter waited as Brano Sev scratched a mole on his cheek, then inhaled deeply through his nose. "Interesting, Comrade Mas. Very interesting."

Peter felt himself flushing with pleasure.

"But . . ."

"Yes?"

Brano Sev adjusted himself on the bench, watching a woman with high heels pass. "In theory, this is a fine idea. Admirable, actually. But, practically, I can see problems."

"Such as?"

"Well, one problem is resources. The workers running this laboratory will have to be taken from the ranks of the Ministry. That's the only way we can be confident of their discretion. How many do you think?"

"Five, maybe six."

"Okay. These Ministry agents will care for some number of patients. Twenty?"

Peter shrugged, then nodded.

"So the Ministry pays for the lives of twenty mental patients and loses five or six trusted agents from the field. For an operation that has a life of one year—two years at most. You understand?"

Peter didn't. "I saw this as going on for much longer than that."

In an uncommon sign of affection, Brano patted Peter's knee.

"If we set up a situation whereby we release teaspoons of information periodically, the agents we're tracking will over time acquire enough information to have the entire picture. One way to delay this moment is to release contradictory information, but at that point their superiors will notice this, and the project will be exposed as a fraud."

Peter squinted at him, taking this in. Then he understood. "I'm sorry, Comrade Colonel. I didn't explain well enough. Each individual agent will not be able to collect more than a few pieces of information, because as soon as he's identified, we will liquidate him. All the West will know is that there is a secret program so important to us that whenever an enemy agent pursues it, he disappears."

Brano Sev stared at him, unblinking. "So the purpose of this operation is to execute foreign agents."

"Yes, Comrade Colonel. Exactly."

Brano Sev watched another passing woman as he chewed the inside of his cheek. "Comrade Mas. While I appreciate your initiative, it's clear that you're living with a fundamental misunderstanding of what we do. Intelligence work is precisely what it says—it's about intelligence. We are not murderers. You may have heard stories during your time with us of operations that ended with the killing of a foreign agent. This happens. But make no mistake—the killing of an enemy agent is seldom the purpose of an operation. When it is, it means the decision has been carefully deliberated over, and all other options have been deemed insufficient." He paused, frowning. "You see, Comrade Mas, the purpose is not to kill the opposition; the purpose is to defeat him. This is not yet a war of attrition. When it becomes that, you'll know, because there will be mushroom clouds on the horizon."

They sat in silence, the flush on Peter's face meaning something entirely different than it had moments before. "Comrade Colonel, I—"

"No," said Brano Sev. "I don't want to hear any more about it. And I don't want anyone else to hear about it. You understand?"

KATJA

•

Istvan returns to the hotel around seven, pink from the sun, and begins telling me about wonderful, hospitable Turks and their oversized hearts. But I'm not interested; I'm famished. I throw him his jacket. "Let's go."

The waiter in the hotel restaurant leads us to a table by the window. He's a tall, thin Turk with heavy eyes and a mustache. Not unattractive.

Istvan's having trouble opening his menu. I wonder if he's drunk and suddenly want to be drunk myself. *"Rakı?"* I ask the waiter.

"With water?"

"No. I want it straight."

The waiter smiles, impressed, at Istvan.

Halfway through my second *rakı*, still waiting on the food, I'm feeling the effects. I begin babbling about Aron. "He's a good man, but simple. I think that's the problem."

Istvan fingers his glass. "I didn't know you were married."

"Is it a problem?"

He shakes his head and leans forward, as if he sympathizes. "What do you mean, though? That he's simple. He's stupid?"

"No," I say, laughing, then stop. Because it's occurred to me that merely calling him "simple" has been enough for a long time. I've never actually defined this word. "His parents," I say, "they were very good to him. They treated him as if he were a prince. *Royalty.* They taught him . . ." I pause. "How to *enjoy* his life. They taught him to appreciate what he has, even me." I reach for my *rakı* and, after draining the glass, my mouth tingling from anise-seed, add, "There have been no tragedies in his life."

Except, I think, *his marriage to me.*

Istvan frowns as I call to the surprised waiter for another. Even I can see I'm making little sense. He says, "You think they were wrong to teach him these things?"

"I think these things are lies. They make a man soft."

"And simple."

"And simple."

"I don't know this man," says Istvan, "but it strikes me that you're confusing optimism with simplicity. In my experience that's just not true. Pessimism—or darkness, or whatever you want to call it—is the simplest thing of all. It's easiest to call the world complicated because it relieves you of responsibility. Optimists must engage the world in all its complexity and still succeed. Pessimists can lounge above the action, can be ironic, can sit with their arms crossed." He pauses, his face very serious. "Pessimists do not take action, which is the only useful thing humans can do. Certainly it's more effective than passive criticism."

During his talk I've been sipping my *rakı* because I have no way of answering his accusations, can only stare at the creases when he smiles, the long lashes that grow from his bright green eyes, the misplaced long hair curling from his left brow, and the way his lips are damp except at the edges, where the dryness is starting to peel.

He nods at my glass, which I'm gripping. "Why are you drinking so much?"

"Because I'm going to have sex with you tonight."

It's the only thing I can think of to unsettle him, and it does.

So there I was. In that apartment on 24th of October Street, telling the old Romanian supervisor that I was a friend of Stanislav's. Which immediately endeared me to her. She began bringing up plates of sarmale and other things with cabbage. Can you imagine? From my life at home, where not even my own mother cared for me, to this. Simply because of a few lies. I was using Stanislav's money. I didn't know what I'd do when it ran out, but for the moment I didn't care. I was Stanislav, you see? And to remind myself I kept his knife with me all the time, inside my jacket, as if his family, too, were mine.

Then there was a knock on the door and I was faced with one of the prettiest young women I'd ever seen.

Yes, Katja Uher. She had seen the light on and wondered if Stanislav had returned. I introduced myself as a close friend, using my real name, and told her lies when she asked what news there was of Stanislav. Her eyes shone when she asked me that. So I told her stories, elaborating on the ones he'd told me. Valor in battle and all that. She was very impressed with her boyfriend. She stayed in Pácin with her family, but most days she took the train into town. I took her out for coffee, convinced her to have a brandy now and then.

You see, it didn't really matter to me that everything was a lie; the fact was that I was happy just to see her face, the way she trusted me implicitly. And for a week, it was . . . it was as if she really were mine. I took her to the cinema, to the puppet shows, and once we even had a picnic. And it didn't even bother me when you showed up, Comrade Sev. Really, it didn't.

Oh, it wasn't simple. You came to the apartment and called me Comrade Private Stanislav Klym and said that I had come to your attention because of my courage in battle. You said that the Ministry was interested in strong young men like myself. It didn't bother me because, ignoring the name, you were right. I am a strong young man, the kind that could be a great help to the Ministry. Besides, you were giving me a plan for the future, something I've never had. Though I told you at first that I needed time to think about it, I knew I'd accept your offer. I had no choice.

Yes, I did tell her, but only that I'd been offered a job. It was an excuse for celebration, and I took her to the Hotel Metropol for dinner, using most of what was left of Stanislav's money.

Right—how do you know this? Yes, afterward, on the walk home, I drew her aside and kissed her.

Is this really important?

No, she did not kiss me back. She became upset and ran away.

I can tell when he reaches orgasm, because men make it known. His silence turns to panting, and I feel him grow inside me. He straightens—at this moment men are the most proud. As if they are onstage, their leakage some kind of gold that only this particular man is capable of producing. Perhaps that's why I push him out before he can stain me.

It doesn't interrupt his performance. He rolls on his back and pulls on himself. At this moment the woman disappears anyway, and there's just a man and his tool and the glory of his mess.

When he's done, he opens his eyes and turns to me, but I've rolled away. I noticed, when I undressed, the expression when he first caught sight of the ragged scar just below my navel, and now it's instinct to hide it from him.

"Katja," he says, then slides up behind me. He's making my buttocks sticky, and that only brings on more tears. "Katja, what's wrong?"

Yes, yes. Okay? I followed her after she ran off. We were in Victory Park, and I caught up with her. I apologized. I said I understood how terrible it was, me being a friend of her fiancé, and perhaps we could put it behind us. She calmed down and said she accepted my apology. Then I asked her if I had a chance. I mean, if Stanislav did not exist.

She frowned—I remember that face clearly. A frown, and then a smile that became a full, terrible laugh. I think she was going to say something, but I didn't find out. I was having trouble hearing her at that point. I grabbed her, she was very light, and dragged her deeper into the park. I threw her down behind some shrubs and began to kiss her. She fought back, I think, but it wasn't very hard to get her out of that skirt and . . .

I'm sorry, I blanked out there. But you know what I mean.

No, actually. I didn't rape her. At first I thought I would, but then I remembered that I had a new life, a new career. One that had to be protected. And this girl, beautiful as she was, she was what one might call a loose end. So I used the knife that I had brought with me from Prague, the one I always carried inside my jacket. I used it on her. Right here.

For the recording, right? I stabbed her in the stomach.

I killed her.

I assume so. It's a big knife, Comrade Sev.

In the darkness, after I get control of my tears and we're just lying there, side by side, Istvan says, "There's a phrase in Islam, *al-hikmat al-majhuulah,* which means 'the unknown wisdom.' It's about those things that Allah does that are beyond our understanding." He pauses. "It's a comforting thing to believe that when the innocent suffer, there's a reason, though we will never understand it." I feel his hot palm on my thigh. "I find it a liberating thought. You?"

He waits for an answer, but I have none to give.

GAVRA

•

They left through the rear of the apartment building, Gavra stomping through the muddy parking lot while Adrian carried his bag a few feet behind, avoiding puddles. Gavra said, "That Trabant. Do you know who it belongs to?"

Adrian didn't.

He'd chosen it because the window was half down. "Don't you have a car out front?" asked Adrian.

"Get in," said Gavra.

He made quick work of the wires beneath the steering wheel, and soon they were moving through the dark streets. Once they reached the highway out of town, Adrian said, "Where?"

"Airport," Gavra muttered.

"Where?"

Gavra looked at him then, as if only now aware he wasn't alone in the car. "Sorry, it's important we leave the country. I'll explain later."

"We're going to Istanbul, aren't we?"

Gavra slowed a little, peering over at him again. "How did you know that?"

Adrian shrugged. "She said you'd take me there."

"She did?"

"She told me lots of things, Gavra. My sister was always right. Always."

KATJA

•

At five in the morning, Istvan's snores wake me. I remain in bed, though, remembering what he said about the idle simplicity of pessimists. He's right. For the past seven years I've let one incident paralyze me. That moment in Victory Park, the sharp cramp of that blade sinking into organs that were made to produce babies, waking up screaming in the Unity Medical emergency ward. Just one night. Years later, I married, but only because Aron Drdova did all the work. I've never really been involved in the marriage, instead standing off to the side with my arms crossed, waiting for its inevitable end. But this is not news—it's something I've known but chosen to ignore as I've watched my husband, with his seemingly endless naive enthusiasm, labor for three years to keep us afloat, to make us into a family. Now he wants what I can't give him—a child—and that makes it all that much worse, because I've never told him why a child is out of the question. He's touched the scar and asked, but I've only given him angry silence.

As I quietly dress in the bathroom, I begin to wonder if this will change anything. After I've done what I've come here to do, will it make any difference to my marriage?

Probably not—but there, again, I'm doing what Istvan accused me of: I'm denying responsibility.

He's still snoring when I get my handbag from the bedside table. It's heavy. I don't look back when I leave; I just go.

The gun in my bag makes me self-conscious in the early-morning crowd as I take the Tünel south to the Galata Bridge. Dark men catch my eye, a few even speak, and after a while they begin to look the same, as if any of them could be the man I slept with last night—the man whose name escapes me for a moment. He's not the first one-night stand I've had since taking my vows to Aron, and probably won't be the last.

No.

On the Galata I smile, because that, again, is the pessimist trap. As things have been, so they will remain. What bullshit.

I'm at the Hotel Erboy by seven, where there's one other person in the lobby. A teenage boy reading a newspaper. The Cyrillic letters on the front confuse me a moment, then I realize it's *Pravda*, ПРАВДА.

For a while—I'm not sure how long, because time has again become strange—I sit in the high-ceilinged lobby, hands on the bag in my lap, looking past him to the elevator in the corner that sometimes spills guests who turn left and descend stairs to the restaurant.

The teenager smiles at me as he turns the page.

I go to the front desk, take a complimentary *Herald Tribune* from a pile, and return to my seat. My English is terrible, and I mostly look at pictures as the sound of morning prayers bleed through the windows.

A wall clock tells me it's a little before eight when I come across the story beneath the face of a fat Turkish man. The story itself, which I translate with great effort, interests me now less than it should.

> Investigators admit to still being unsure about the cause of the explosion that downed Turkish Airlines Flight 54 just over a week ago, in the early hours of Wednesday, April 23, killing all 68 passengers and crew.
>
> "That it was a bomb placed by the Army of the Liberation of Armenia, we know, but whether its explosion was on purpose or the result of bad wiring is still being investigated," said Istanbul police captain Talip Evren at a press conference Thursday morning.

At that point I stop reading, because the man known as Ludvík Mas is exiting the elevator and descending to the restaurant. It's time for his complimentary breakfast.

PETER

•

Sitting over his sparse continental breakfast, Peter found himself dreaming of the afternoon flight home. Only a few hours to go. He had lain in bed last night, uncomfortable, wanting only to proceed to the room with his hunting knife and take care of that Martrich queer as soon as possible. But he had to wait. The flight left at eleven, and he would have to do the job just beforehand, to assure that no one alerted the border guards and kept him in this miserable city.

An hour ago, Brano Sev had called to explain that, despite his best efforts, he had found no record of another agent who would have used the Dutch chapel pistol. But he assured Peter that he would continue his investigations until he'd uncovered the culprit.

"You don't really care," Peter said.

"Excuse me, Comrade Mas?"

"Come on, Brano. You've never forgiven me for going over your head with Room 305."

Brano sighed. "I don't hold grudges."

"I'm glad to hear that, Comrade Sev."

"I still feel, however, that the project was never of any political value. I think its history has proven that."

Peter grunted. He was so far from being Brano's protégé, and it had been such a long time since he'd had to listen to the old man's antiquated ideals. "Brano, the political died in 1968 in Prague. Since then, socialism has become entirely personal. Room 305 may have had no political benefits, but it certainly had personal benefits."

"Like your career."

"For example."

"Good day."

"Good day, Comrade Sev."

Over breakfast he remembered that other meeting in 1972, a week after Brano's refusal to consider his plan. Peter had gone straight to the Comrade Lieutenant General and received an enthusiastic response. The next day, Brano cornered him in the Yalta lobby. *Remember what I told you, Ludvík. Mushroom clouds on the horizon. Some of us don't actually want that.*

Over time their relationship had thawed again, each going about his own work, until Brano's new protégé, that Gavra Noukas, stuck his nose into the great debacle that was Zrinka Martrich.

They'd brought her to the clinic—not in Rokošyn, because that complex had already been destroyed, but a warehouse outside of Uzhorod—and treated her the same way they treated all the other delusionals they'd collected from around the country. Food, guarded walks in the fenced grounds, and sleep. The only plan was to keep them alive.

She was prettier than most—all the Ministry guards noticed this—and very even-tempered. She caused no trouble and, until a year into her stay, didn't even bother to speak with her guards. When she did, it was to Petrov, an old Ministry hand nearing retirement, who tried to take her by force in the interview room.

Neither knew they were being recorded by a video camera Peter had recently had installed, but when Petrov stepped out into the corridor and placed his Walther PP against his own teeth and pulled the trigger, Peter demanded to see the tape.

Petrov's recorded voice was not unlike his own back in 1968, when he cornered the fiancée of the man he had killed in Prague, but Zrinka's reaction was entirely different from Katja Uher's. When Zrinka pushed him back, she spoke calmly, just a few words about Petrov's son, Sasha.

Sasha will never understand, but the rest of the world does. The rest of the world knows.

And Petrov went quiet. He walked into the corridor and closed the door. Zrinka crossed her arms . . . as if *waiting*. When the gunshot sounded, muffled by the door, she didn't even jump.

They began the first actual tests the clinic had ever run. Zrinka would not perform for them, so Peter sent in another guard, Dubi, whom they rushed to stop before he cut his own throat with a knife. Dubi spent the next week in a hospital bed, sedated, until finally making it to the window and throwing himself out.

Zrinka Martrich would perform, but only by force.

That was when Peter looked into her file and learned of a brother living in the Capital.

It was simple extortion. If she would go along with a test run on a Swedish Interpol official they wanted dead, then her brother could live. He smiled at her across the interview room's table.

Stay away from my brother.

Only you can save him now.

You're a true shit. That's plain as day.

Such language!

She paused. *Why do you want the man dead?*

That's our business.

She squinted a moment, her bloodshot eyes focused beyond him, then relaxed. *He's investigating something, isn't he? The funding of terrorists. Yes. By our government. By you.*

Peter almost dropped to the floor right there. This woman terrified him, but he got control of himself, climbed to his feet, and left.

Zrinka spent the next two days in her room considering the plan. On the video, she appeared to be sleeping most of the time. She ignored her food. Then, finally, she sat up straight and called for him.

What happens after I've done it?

Your brother will be allowed to live in peace.

She nodded. *And me?*

We'll see then.

To Peter's surprise, she agreed. Then she said, *Would you like to know about an impending terrorist attack?*

He didn't know what to say, so he just nodded.

There is a group of Turkish Armenians, led by a man named Norair Tigran in Istanbul, who are planning to hijack a plane from our country. They haven't yet decided what plane, or when, but there's one person they'll listen to. Wilhelm Adler.

That, finally, was enough to force him down into a chair. *How do you know about Adler?*

I know lots of things, Peter Husák.

He stood again, deeply frightened now, and backed out of the room.

"More?" asked a white-smocked woman with an aluminum teapot.

He watched her pour, then brought the cup to his lips.

From what they'd been able to learn, Zrinka Martrich controlled people not only by the words she spoke but also by the tone of her voice, which was why Peter went through the files of handicapped Ministry thugs and found Ádám, a deaf ex-boxer from Krosno, who was told nothing of what would happen on the plane.

Only now was it evident that the bitch had been manipulating him all along. She had told him about the Armenians because she—somehow—knew that he would alter his plan. While she would still be sent to kill the Swede, she would have an additional, surprise task. She knew this. She knew he would call Wilhelm Adler to tell the Armenians to hijack the plane she would be taking to Istanbul. She knew he would supply them with explosives. And she knew that Peter believed that, placed in the middle of such a debacle, she would use her abilities to solve the problem.

He could not explain the *how* of her abilities. He only knew that she had been smarter than him. She had talked him into arranging her suicide.

At the time, though, he'd only been amazed by his good fortune.

Then, a fireball over Bulgaria.

But *why?* While Zrinka Martrich certainly had the ability to bring down the plane, he doubted she would kill sixty-eight people simply in order to undermine Peter's career. If she really wanted to get at him, she would have convinced the terrorists to fly to the West, and then she'd be free. Then again, she knew that if she did that, he would kill her brother, Adrian. She couldn't have known that he would kill him anyway.

Yet if she knew so many other things, how could she not know this?

He'd considered at first that Brano Sev was behind the explosion, but even Brano would not have gone so far. Theirs was not yet a war of attrition.

Despite everything, it had been a good run. Three years of a perfectly oiled trap that lured enemy agents into their territory and then crushed them. Unlike Romania or Poland, theirs was a country that the West would think twice about before invading with intelligence agents.

And he still had his career. Room 305 by now had multiple departments controlling many types of disruption services; there was plenty of work for him to return to. This particular department, dealing with Rokošyn, would be quietly covered up, the last remaining threads disposed of, and he could go on to the next project. Or he could take a well-earned vacation, take Ilza and Iulian to the Black Sea. They'd spent too long in the cloistered world he'd built for them; it was time to show them around.

As he climbed the stairs to the lobby and took the vibrating elevator back up to his room, he again thought through the mechanism of Adrian Martrich's death. It was simple. In a few hours, the desk clerk would call up to their room and say that a package was being delivered for Gavra Noukas and needed to be signed for. A package from Brano Sev. While Gavra was downstairs, looking for the absent deliveryman, Peter would be upstairs. Gavra would return to a dead lover.

Peter stepped out of the elevator and unlocked his door, glancing once up the empty corridor, then went inside. As he packed his bag, he began humming unconsciously, then realized what it was. Mozart's "Turkish Rondo." He even laughed to himself. A bit of Mozart to see him off.

From the side pocket of his suitcase he took out the hunting knife, which he'd kept sharp over the years. He'd used it twice in the last three years, to dispose of a French agent and an American one. Now, when he looked at it, he could hardly remember the young private he'd taken it from.

What he did remember clearly, and could never forget, was the lesson of that night. He'd felt the unarticulated knowledge on the long train ride from Prague to the Capital, felt it again after that final night with the girl, but only during that week answering Brano Sev's questions did the words gather and give voice to the most important lesson he would ever learn: The first step to complete independence, the first step to asserting your free will, is to seek out and bring to light all your own darkest secrets. You must act on your bleakest impulses before true freedom becomes yours, before you can take control of your life.

Sometimes he considered writing this down.

There was a knock at the door. Instinctively, he slipped the knife under the wardrobe, where he kept his money, then stepped over to the door.

"Yes?"

"Sir, for you a letter," a woman said in difficult English.

"Slip it under."

The woman paused, then said, "Is big. Is too big, sir."

"Okay. Just a second." He turned the lock, then opened the door.

The woman looking back at him was not Turkish. She was white, attractive despite the heavy, sleep-deprived eyes, and familiar. But from where? He reached to accept the letter, staring into those eyes, but there was no letter at all.

KATJA

•

I shoot him once in the stomach when he opens the door. A sharp explosion rings in my ears. The recoil goes through to my elbow, jerking it. He stumbles back a few feet, then falls as if he's slipped on a banana peel.

Really, that's how it looks.

Lying on the floor, he covers the hole in his stomach with a hand, but the blood comes out between his fingers. His face—up close it's older than I remember; it's been through things—is contorted, his lips loose and flapping with his quick, stunned breaths.

That's when my head clears. Cordite burns in my nostrils as I check the empty corridor, then come inside and close the door. He tries to cry for help, but he can't get enough breath for anything more than quiet groans and the occasional whisper.

"What?" I say, standing over him. "Did you say something?"

It's difficult to read that twisted face. There's pain, but it seems to be masking something. Surprise, perhaps.

He whispers, "What do you want?"

It's just like the voice on the recording, just like the voice I remember.

But he's asked me a question, and I'm not sure what I want. A part of me wonders if I'm done now, if seven years have led to that one bullet, and perhaps I should just leave.

He coughs, shooting pink spittle across the beige carpet.

I open his suitcase on the bed. Nothing except clothes.

"Money," he whispers.

I come around to look at him. "Money?"

His eyes are very large. Blood drains from the corner of his lips as he says, "Wardrobe . . . under." Then: "Hospital."

I don't know what's gotten into me. I've shot a man in the stomach, but there's a hysterical lightness to my step as I hop over him to look beneath the wardrobe. This lightness will leave me, I know, but now I'm almost giddy. Crouching, I find a plastic bag filled with Deutschmarks and, beside it, a hunting knife.

Only when I pick it up and look at the hawk burned into its leather sheath does the adrenaline lessen. The dying man is now trying to roll onto his side.

"Hospital," he whispers.

Time slows again as I remember this knife, the hilt that I saw coming out of my stomach. Stanislav's knife, the one his father, weeping, presented him before he was shipped off to Prague. I was there to see the exchange. So were my mother and father. We all drank plum brandy.

"I have family," he whispers.

I crawl over to him because my legs are not working well. He's rolled to his side in the pool of his blood. I'm in that pool myself, my forearms sticky.

As if he can understand, I say, "Maybe it's too simple, but yes, I blame you for everything."

He blinks and whispers: "Who . . . are . . . you?"

I don't understand, because it's an impossible question. He must know me. How could I carry his face with me for seven years and he just—

I unsheathe the knife.

"No," he whispers, his confused eyes growing again.

I climb behind him, place the point against his Adam's apple and my knee behind his head. He tries to swat it with his hands, but his arms won't rise that far.

Just before I push it in, he says the word that will remain with me for some time to come, in that whispered, dying tone.

He says, "Katja."

From the look on your face I'm guessing you didn't know what I did to her. If so, you wouldn't have called me here. But let me tell you this, Comrade Sev. I'm not random. I'm a man who knows what is required at any moment. You told me that if I was interested in working for the Ministry, I should meet you in Victory Park on Friday. I was interested. I am interested. And I knew that if I was to be of proper service to the Ministry, I had to tie up my loose ends. An agent is no good if there are others out there who wish him ill, who know too much about him. No. It's unacceptable. So that's what I did. I tied up my loose ends. I got rid of that girl. And now I'm here, ready to serve the Ministry with all the cunning I can muster.

GAVRA

•

They got out at the same sidewalk where Libarid Terzian stood when he waved good-bye to his family for the last time, six days before. Adrian carried his little bag, but Gavra carried nothing. He opened the same door for Adrian that Libarid held open for Adrian's sister, and, like Zrinka, Adrian smiled.

Gavra paused before continuing to the TisAir desk. He scanned the departures lounge, trying to find familiar faces. Then he noticed the sloped gray-haired Ministry man smoking by the gift shop, but he was more interested in flirting with the young, bored girl who worked the shop than watching out for people trying to escape their country.

Gavra crossed the faux-marble floor to the desk while Adrian took a seat in the waiting area. Gavra bought two tickets for the nine thirty flight, and as he returned his face became very red as he finally understood what he was doing. But he didn't say anything to Adrian about it. He just handed over a ticket and explained, "It would be best if we went through passport control separately."

"That's fine."

Gavra went through first and waited on the other side of the glassed-in desk as Adrian handed over his passport. Gavra was breaking every known rule this evening, and he couldn't explain why. Brano had always been right—he was young and sentimental. He wasn't cut out for this work. Anyone who would throw away his career because of a man he'd known only a few days had no respect for his career. That was logical. What did he expect to gain from this? A lifetime of happiness with a man he hardly knew?

As Adrian joined him with a smile, Gavra knew that he could have taken care of this back at Adrian's apartment. It would have been difficult; it would have haunted him for weeks—perhaps months—but at some unknown point in the future he would have woken to a clean conscience, settling into the comfort of knowing that what he had done was simply a part of duties. As some people grasp hold of religion, Gavra would learn to grasp hold of the ideals of the Ministry.

But now—now he'd killed any chance for that kind of faith.

So he continued without thinking. It was better that way. He waited silently with Adrian at the gate, then took a seat with him just over the wing. He closed his eyes as the plane ascended.

Finally, when they were over Romania, Gavra whispered, "What else did she tell you?"

Adrian yawned into the back of his hand. "Excuse me." He covered Gavra's hand with his own. "She told me about this, that you would take me to Istanbul. She said I should go, because if I stayed I would die."

Gavra shook his head. "I just don't understand any of this. How can someone know these things?"

Zrinka's brother took a breath. "It's hard to explain. She tried many times, when we were children, but it's hard." He paused. "You and I, we've long ago accepted that there are things we will never know. We're like characters in a Tolstoy novel—we know things are happening to other people, but we don't know what those things are, or why those people do what they do. Zrinka, though, she's like the reader of our novel."

"But you're not telling me *how*."

"Okay. Think of it like mathematics. Statistics. What's the probability that if I say something to you, you'll do something else?"

"I don't know."

"I would know if I knew all the things that had happened to you up to this point in your life. And I mean *everything*. Then I could say with precision what you'd do next."

"With precision?"

"To go along with this idea, you have to rid yourself of one concept."

"What?"

"Free will."

Gavra began to feel a little dumb.

"Or better yet," said Adrian, "go ahead and believe in it, but remember that even free will is predictable."

"Which one is it?" said Gavra. "Does it exist or not?"

Adrian shrugged. "I don't know. All I know is that Zrinka knew what I or our parents would do next. As she got older, she knew more."

"But she didn't know everything that had happened to them up to that point. She couldn't."

Adrian paused, as if this were a good point. "Well, take that idea and turn it around. You meet someone, see how he's acting, what he looks like, how old he is, what kind of language he uses. Then you can work backward to find out what's happened to him. Psychology does this in a rudimentary way, but so simply that all they can say are things like *You had a trauma when you were a child*. Well, who hasn't?"

Gavra nodded.

"Put those together. If I can tell your whole past from who you are now, and then with that information predict what you'll do next, can even influence what you do or feel or think next, then you have a picture of what my sister was capable of."

Adrian waited, watching Gavra absorb this, then confused him further by pushing it to its limit.

"There's more. If you're very good at this, you're able to understand people you've never even met. For someone you *have* met to act this way or that, he had to have been influenced by contact with *this* kind of person, because only one kind of person, or one combination of people, could have affected that person in this exact way. And you learn *that* person's past, and future, just as if you had met him personally. And so it grows. Before long, there exists a vast web of people whose actions you can predict. That is, if you can keep it all straight in your head."

Gavra whispered, "You're talking about omniscience."

"Something like that. But not omnipotence. Certainly not that."

Gavra still wasn't convinced, but he had spent enough time managing interrogations to know how to follow a subject's line of reasoning, no matter how absurd it seemed.

"That," said Adrian, "is why she was able to know that I would meet you. She knew Ludvík Mas, so she knew Brano Sev. And because she knew *him,* she also knew you." He paused. "She knew what Brano Sev needed to know."

"That Ludvík Mas knew about the hijacking. But why did he need to know that?"

"I don't know. I just know it's important for me, and for you, that he know."

Gavra rubbed his eyes. This line of reasoning was logical but impossible to digest. "I don't know," he said.

"You don't have to know. I know. My sister, as I've said before, was a saint. She spent her life since the age of fifteen suffering in hospitals and being studied and then manipulated. All to protect me."

"How was she manipulated?"

"They gained her cooperation by threatening my life. She told me that."

Gavra peered over the headrests up the length of the plane. Stewardesses in blue caps were serving drinks to businessmen in first class. And here he was, listening to a story that was beyond his capacity to comprehend.

LIBARID

•

"*Everyone remain* calm!" says Emin Kazanjian, waving his brief-case detonator at the head of the aisle. "If you stay calm, everyone will survive this trip!" The other three hijackers have taken positions throughout the plane, so they can see its length and breadth as Emin retreats, with the help of a terrified stewardess, to the cockpit.

Zrinka sits up and whispers to Libarid, "The one closest to us—you see his arm?"

Libarid's not interested in what she has to say, not now, but he looks anyway at the small man in the aisle with shirtsleeves and an old Tokarev pistol. Down his forearm are three long, parallel scars. "Yes," he mutters.

He doesn't know why Zrinka continues to speak, but she does. "His name is Jirair, and he was tortured by Turkish police in Is-tanbul, three years ago. They brought him in on trumped-up charges of robbery, but they in fact believed he was a terrorist. He wasn't, but after the experience he became one. Ironic, isn't it?"

Libarid looks at her. "How the hell do you know that?"

"I told you," she says. "I have a knack for suppositions. Some-times it serves me well. For example, I knew this plane was going to be hijacked."

"Everyone *quiet!*" says the one nearest them—Jirair.

Libarid lowers his voice. "I saw you. You were talking with that first guy. In the airport."

"I needed to get to know him."

"*What?*"

"Don't worry," she says, a vague smile playing on her lips. "It'll all be over soon enough. You'll be in sunny Istanbul, and free."

Zrinka places a hand on the armrest to get up, but Libarid grabs her elbow and pulls her back down. "You're staying right here."

"Am I?" That smile again.

"Explain to me what's going on."

"A test," she says. "I'm being tested. But I've had enough of tests. I've had years of them, and this is where it's going to end. I could just have them take the plane somewhere else—to Egypt, maybe—but I won't have my brother pay for my selfishness. Be-sides, there's always another side that wants to use you."

"You're not making things any clearer."

"It's doesn't matter, Libarid. Zara will at least be happy you've survived the flight. And these guys will treat you well; though you're nothing like them, you're Armenian."

"I'm not so different. I've hated the Turks as well."

Zrinka opens her mouth, a peculiar expression crossing her face. When she speaks, it's a stunned whisper. "No, you don't hate them."

"I *did,*" he said. "They killed most of my family. Made refugees of my mother and me."

Her mouth works air again. "But I didn't *know*."

For an instant, Libarid forgets the situation they're in. "Christ, you're strange."

"But I'm sure it's the same," she says, nodding as if to reassure herself. "Yes. Now let go of my arm."

As if it were controlled by the tone of her voice, Libarid's hand opens up, and Zrinka stands. Jirair rushes up, swinging his pistol around. "Sit!"

Zrinka smiles at him. "I need to speak to Emin."

"You don't—"

But she interrupts, pointing at the marks on his arm. "His name was Talip Evren. He was short and fat, and he used a ceremonial Bedouin knife he got when he was in the army. He used the knife because it reminded him of when he was young and fit and strong. And you're here because there was something wicked about him that keeps you moving even now, three years later."

Jirair looks down at the marks on his forearm, then back at her.

"Emin," she says.

Libarid watches as the small man deflates slightly, his shoulders drooping, his pistol hanging beside his hip. He's very close, and for an instant Libarid believes he can reach out and snatch the gun from him. But he doesn't. He's thinking of the various repercussions that could follow, gunfights in this enclosed space, Zrinka getting shot, or, worse, himself being killed. The scenarios flicker through his mind slowly, retarded by fear, and Jirair and Zrinka are already walking up to the cockpit when he realizes he should have tried it—tried *something*.

Then they're at the door, and just before entering, Zrinka turns to look at him with her pale eyes. The serene smile hasn't left her face, and then she winks at him and mouths, *It's okay*.

Jirair opens the door to the cockpit, and Libarid can hear Emin, from inside, shout in Armenian, "What is this?"

The door closes.

Libarid stares hard at the door, then at the deaf state security man who turns to peer back at him, confused. *It's okay,* she said, but it's not okay. As a young refugee, Libarid learned that other people have no power to help you. They may believe they can right what's fallen apart, but they're fooling themselves. What is good for you, only you can do.

He turns to the hijacker across the next set of seats and calls in Armenian, "Excuse me, can I use the bathroom?"

He's a tall, gangly man, also with scars that mark the side of his face. One scar has split the corner of his wide mustache. He raises his gun and frowns. "What?"

Libarid smiles. Again in Armenian: "I'm sorry, but I don't want to wet my pants."

The hijacker looks across the plane to the other one at the front of Libarid's aisle, who shrugs. The first one nods, and the second comes back to walk Libarid from his seat to the toilet. At the bathroom door, he asks Libarid, "You're Armenian?"

"*Aayo.* Family was from Vaspurakan. We were around for the slaughter."

The hijacker inhales, his smooth face looking very young and innocent to Libarid. "Nineteen fifteen, April. You must have been a baby."

"I was young."

Libarid locks the door and stares into the mirror. That brief childhood in Armenia is hardly a memory to him at his age. When he was young, memories of Turkish soldiers marching the men of the village away, gathering families, drowning them in the local lake—they gave him an immature, violent courage. But over the years, after the death of his mother, his hatred of Turks was too exhausting to sustain. Then, once he'd acquired a wife and child—a family—he became more careful. Now, staring at himself, he can see this. It's made him a less effective militiaman, one with too many worries and, at times, a crippling fear of death.

But now the situation is different. Libarid has kept up with the stories of various Armenian acts around the world, and their perpetrators' awkward names: the Prisoner Gourgen Yanikian Group, the Armenian Secret Army for the Liberation of Armenia, and now simply the Army of the Liberation of Armenia. Bombs placed in tourist offices in New York, Paris, and Beirut. The hatred he once owned is alive in these people, and he knows from his own experience what that can lead to. It's a suicidal urge. If he doesn't act, his freedom from his family won't mean a thing.

So he looks around at the minimalist airline toilet for something to use. The cabinets are filled with paper products, and beneath the sink are extra rolls of toilet paper. The toilet itself has only a lid, but beside it, on the wall, is a two-foot-long aluminum bar to hold on to during turbulence. He tugs on it, and the plastic wall bends. The bar is held on each side by screwed-in metal brackets, but with some effort one of them pops free, and he slides the aluminum bar under his slacks, the bottom secured by the elastic of his sock, so that the bar is held loosely along the inside of his calf.

He checks his red face in the mirror, takes a breath, and opens the door.

His guard walks behind him back to his seat, and as they approach Zrinka's large, deaf guard, Libarid mouths his instructions.

Five minutes, we both take them. You stand first.

The guard, surprised, nods and looks at his wristwatch.

KATJA

•

The sunlight ruins me. It's inescapable. Even when I find a crevice between buildings, the light clings to the shadows, and I search for a closed door to hide behind. The first door is a teashop with pillows around low tables and dark men hunched in the darkness, whispering. That is, until I enter, when they all look up from their reveries, confused.

I tried not to run out of the hotel. I ran from the room, then stood in the empty corridor with blood on my knees and hands and blouse, the knife still in my hand. Then, in a moment of sudden fatigue, I stepped back inside and closed the door, lucky that the guests were all gone, eating late breakfasts or gazing at Istanbul's sights. I stepped over the dead man, sat on the bed, and closed my eyes.

I don't know how long it took me, in the darkness of my head, to decide what to do, but when I came out of it I found myself undressing.

I tried to ignore him as I washed my hands and went through the wardrobe and put on his undershirt and then tried pants, but they wouldn't stretch over my hips. So I put my own back on and found a long raincoat with large pockets. I dropped the pistol and the knife into a plastic trash bag from the bathroom and slipped it into one pocket. Into the other went my crumpled, bloodstained blouse. I found an inner pocket to hold the Deutschmarks. Then I looked around, at everything except the body.

Before leaving, I admittedly squatted beside Peter Husák again, just outside the pool of blood, and gazed into that flaccid, blood-smeared face. That stupid little mustache.

I spat on it.

Only then was I able to walk calmly out of the hotel.

I walked eastward. Up a narrow cobblestone street, jumping aside to avoid cars and lumbering tour buses. Up, pouring sweat under the overcoat, until my calves hurt, burning away all thoughts. In an open square I saw men washing themselves in fountains.

Then down, almost tripping on the stones as I followed baffling curves.

Trees covered me at some point, and then I reached the water. A perfect horizontal line. Water above; road below. In the distance, ships and Asia. I sprinted across the road to a shore of large rocks. Just at the water, feet wet, I collapsed and threw the blouse and the pistol into the Bosphorus. The knife, though—I held on to that. I looked around finally, but I'd been alone all along.

It was walking back through these choked, confused streets that ruined my shaky calm. The heat and the weathered faces and the unsettling songs of prayer that burst from rooftops like the scorn of God. The sun.

So I've stepped into this dark cavern of men over steaming cups. The last place I want to be. I find a pillow at an empty table and try to smile at the gaunt waiter with the long sideburns. "*Rakı,* please," I say.

He frowns, then shakes his head vigorously.

"*Çay,*" he says, then: "*Chai.* Tea."

"No alcohol?"

He shakes his head again.

"Oh." With effort I climb back to my feet. All those mustached faces follow me as I walk back out into the light.

LIBARID

•

He stretches out his leg under the next seat so the aluminum bar won't cut into his skin, and as the hijacker returns to his post near Zrinka's guard, Jirair leaves the cockpit and comes back to him.

The hijacker leans close and speaks in Armenian. "Who's that girl?"

"I don't know. I'd never met her before."

"Is she a spy?"

Libarid looks up at this earnest, confused face. He's young, maybe twenty-eight, and Libarid almost feels sympathy for him. "If she is, I wouldn't know."

"She's frightening."

When Jirair straightens and steps back, Libarid draws the bar from his pants leg, watching the bald head of Zrinka's guard, and wonders if he'll ever see his family again. Then it hits him—he wasn't going to see them again anyway. A simple realization, but only now, minutes before risking his life, does the reality of never seeing his son again crystallize in his head. He's spent the last months and years thinking of what he would gain by leaving, and that he'd only lose the tedium, as if a life lived alone is a joyride.

Unbelievable, he thinks as he listens to Jirair breathe heavily a couple paces behind him. Zara learned from her Bible that what we do affects others to a degree we can never predict. What would his abandonment do to Vahe?

What kind of man is he?

He forces the question from his mind, because Zrinka's big guard is standing, reaching out.

"Sit down," Jirair says, then takes a step forward. Zrinka's guard reaches for the one nearest him, a quick arm around the neck, and Libarid swings the aluminum bar into Jirair's legs. The Armenian tumbles, and Libarid, low, throws himself on top of him.

There's a gunshot from the third one, in the other aisle, and screams follow. Libarid brings the bar down on the back of Jirair's head with strength—he feels the skull give. Ahead, the Ministry man has broken the other's neck and is rising with his pistol, shooting over heads at the third one. One bullet throws the hijacker back on top of a screaming woman, while a second snaps through a window.

A great sucking sound.

Libarid's ears pop and he can't hear a thing as, crouching, he runs forward. The floor tilts and he stumbles past the guard, who's lying with blood pulsing from his shoulder but alive. From seats, disconnected arms reach out to grab him. He pushes past them to the cockpit door, where a stewardess is screaming something he can't hear.

Then he pulls open the door and sees her. Those eyes. And for the first time, there's something like surprise all over that beautiful face. Surprise and real, clear terror.

GAVRA

•

Gavra hailed a taxi from the sidewalk outside Atatürk International Airport and took Adrian to the only Istanbul hotel he'd
ever stayed in, the Erboy. On the ride, Adrian acted like a giddy
child as he peered out the window at the ship-lights on the Sea of
Marmara. "My first time here," he said. "But you know it pretty
well, I guess."

"I know it well enough," Gavra said, though at that moment he
felt like he didn't know it at all. The dilapidated buildings they
passed, and then the Aya Sofia—they all seemed different now.

He registered them at the front desk, while Adrian picked up a
complimentary copy of the *Herald Tribune*. Then they went up to
the room, number 305. Gavra had noticed it on the key ring, then
in the elevator looked at it again to be sure. He felt an urge to return to the front desk and ask for a different room but changed
his mind. He didn't want to be superstitious.

While Adrian showered, Gavra opened the window and looked
down İbni Kemal, the busy restaurant row behind the hotel. He
still had no answer to the *why* of what he was doing. Did he really
believe that Zrinka Martrich possessed the powers her brother had

told him about? He didn't know, but if it were true—if he did believe—then what about Adrian himself? Was it possible he had the power to influence people around him? Could he influence Gavra into committing an act he still could not entirely understand?

Adrian came out of the bathroom wrapped in a white towel, his wet hair flat over his forehead. "What?" he said.

"They're going to come after us," said Gavra. "Ludvík Mas, the man who tried to kill you before. He's going to come after us."

"Don't worry about it."

"Why not?"

"Because we all did what we were supposed to do."

Gavra sat on a chair as Adrian used the towel on his hair, standing naked by the bed. "What does that mean?"

"You haven't been listening, dear," said Adrian. "I did what she asked me to do. And you did what I asked you to do—you passed on the message to Brano Sev. She told me that if these things were done, you and I would be in no danger here."

"Why not?"

He shrugged and brought down the towel. "Because she said so. Just accept it. You and I, we're on vacation. That's all."

"How do you know she wasn't wrong? Or that she didn't lie?"

Adrian went back to drying his hair. "My sister's entire life since the age of fifteen was about protecting me. She was more of a mother than my mother ever was."

Gavra unbuttoned his shirt. "I need a shower, too."

"Water's hot," Adrian said as he unfolded the newspaper and began to read.

Under the water, he worked again through all the details of the sister who had protected her brother since the age of fifteen. He pictured young Adrian and his pretty sister living in a clapboard house full of fear and pain.

"Listen to this," Adrian said from the other side of the curtain.

"What?"

He read from the newspaper. "Last Saturday's speech at the Interpol International Conference on Crime and Cooperation in Istanbul by Swedish delegate Roland Adelsvärd continues to send ripples through the international arena. Adelsvärd accused Soviet Bloc countries of funding terrorist cells throughout Western Europe and America in order to disrupt the functions of democratic nations. Of particular focus was General Secretary Tomiak Pankov of—" He stopped. "Are you listening?"

"Yeah," said Gavra as the water cooled over his skin. When Adrian continued reading, though, he stopped listening. The Swede was talking about what everyone in the Ministry knew but chose not to discuss, because no one wanted to know. Room 305. Disruption Services.

"Amazing, huh?" said Adrian.

"Yeah," Gavra repeated.

By the time he turned off the water and wrapped the hotel towel around himself, something had occurred to him. He dripped all over the carpet when he came out to find Adrian stretched out under the sheets, the paper turned to the sports page. Gavra said, "It was you."

"What was me?"

"Your parents. They didn't kill themselves, did they? You did it, and your sister spent her life protecting you."

Adrian raised himself on his elbows and cocked his head. "What?"

"You heard me."

Adrian slid back down, sighed, and spoke to the ceiling. "At first, she believed she had done it. She really did. She believed that she had influenced me to kill them. Unconsciously or consciously, it didn't matter. But that's not true. I did what I felt was necessary. And she did what she thought was necessary as well. She allowed herself to be taken away. A saint, like I keep telling you."

"But you were . . . what? Eleven?"

"Thirteen."

"And you . . . ?"

"They had passed out in the backyard, okay? Passed out drunk. I just made it look like they'd done it to themselves."

Gavra sat on the bed beside Adrian's feet. "You hid it from me."

"I was supposed to hide it. For the moment, at least. I really wish you hadn't figured it out."

"Why not?"

Adrian shrugged at the ceiling lamp. "I must have said too much. You weren't supposed to find out."

"*Why?*"

He sat up, staring past Gavra at the mirror on the wall. "But I didn't say too much." He looked at Gavra, his features twisted. "That was a *guess,* wasn't it?"

"A hunch."

"I can't believe it," he said, frowning. "She was *wrong.* Which means . . ." He started rubbing his ear. "The plane."

Gavra stood again. He wished this man—this childhood murderer—would make sense. "*What about the plane?*"

Adrian peered at his reflection. "It's possible . . . possible, mind you . . . that she made a mistake on the plane. I'd never considered that. Which would explain why it . . ."

"Blew up."

Adrian nodded. "Do you see what I mean? There's so much for her to keep track of. So many people, variables . . . so many unforeseen chance events. The brain isn't wired for that." He lay down again. "And now this. Our parents. You were *not* supposed to find out yet. We were supposed to have more time."

This was enough. Gavra climbed on the bed and pinned Adrian down. Their faces were very close. "Stop speaking in riddles."

"Kiss me first."

Gavra did so. "Now tell me why I shouldn't know about your parents. What difference does it make now? You're not going to jail for it."

Adrian cleared his throat. "Because, my dear, I am a murderer. And that knowledge will change everything for you. Not yet, no, but soon. The love you feel for me—and if she was right, it *is* love—will crumble." He paused. "Before this moment, I was elusive, a mystery to you. But that allure will start to fade, and you'll begin to wonder why you've thrown away your life, and your good career, for a simple butcher like me." He swallowed, blinking. "You'll think back. You'll start to imagine me, as a child, murdering my parents. And you have a good imagination. You'll wonder what kind of creature could do such a thing and then live his life as if nothing had happened. I won't be a mystery anymore; I'll be a monster." He swallowed again, a sound like choking, then whispered, "And then, my dear, you'll do what you were ordered to do by Brano Sev. You'll kill me."

"No," said Gavra, because that was unimaginable. He kissed Adrian's forehead. "I'd never kill you."

Adrian smiled. "We can hope she's wrong about that, too, can't we?"

They kissed, and neither was surprised when Gavra's tears dripped onto Adrian's cheeks.

"It's all right," said Zrinka's brother. "Really it is. By that time we'll have had a good run, such a good run. You'll have enough memories to last you a lifetime. Because in the end, a life doesn't require so many, does it?"

ZRINKA

•

The details. The details. If only I'd let that fat guard rape me, then we wouldn't be here. But my reaction was a reflex, as with any woman, and I told Petrov that I knew about Sasha, that we all knew that he had fondled his son years ago. He believed no one knew about that. But I did. I know everything.

That's not pride talking.

As Jirair walks me to the cockpit I work back over the details. I've called the hotel and Adrian, yes, I've told him everything. That side is taken care of. If he follows the instructions—*if*—then my brother will be free. He'll be liberated. And Gavra will remember that he once loved a beautiful man who slipped away in the night. Like names on a list, I can see them all so clearly that it cannot be wrong. Peter Husák, the easiest of all to control—the liars always are—will lie dead in his hotel. A kind of liberation as well. He will get what he deserves from the person he deserves it from—Katja Drdova—and in the process save my brother. She will save herself as well.

And this militiaman, Libarid—a good choice. A frightened

man will do nothing, will sit and remain calm and make no trouble because he wants his own liberation too much. He wants the peace of solitude and many many women. But the hatred—the family history in Turkey—how did I not see that? No, it won't change a thing. He's just right, so at the cockpit door I give him a smile and mouth *It's okay*, just to let him know he's the right one for me.

And we're inside.

"What is this?" says Emin in his own language, turning from the radio and ending contact with the ground.

Oh, the fear is everywhere. Emin is covered in it, poor man. This will sicken him. This act. Afterward he will no longer trust himself, and he will land smoothly at Atatürk International and give himself and his men up. After a childhood like his, and then killing a woman like me, everything will be undermined. *I hate myself*, he will say, just like I say it every day.

I've got it right. I swear I've got it right.

If the numbers are right.

They are. They must be.

But there's so much to keep track of.

The two Turkish pilots are no trouble. None. They're crouched in their seats wishing for nothing more than to see their children again as Emin grips that suitcase with the button on its handle that, if pressed, will send a brief shortwave pulse to the gray suitcase in the baggage hold. To the blasting cap embedded in the six pounds of C-4 explosive Peter Husák passed to him in the restaurant of the Hotel Metropol.

He repeats himself. "Jirair, what is this?"

What I've said has terrified poor Jirair. *How can she know? What is this woman?* So he will leave us in peace for it to be done.

"This woman, she needs to speak with you."

"What?" says Emin. He's had trouble keeping control of his frightened men these last several days and says what I know he'll say: "Get her out of here. I don't have time for her."

Because he doesn't remember me. Because all I said to him was *Excuse me, but are you Armenian? I have a cousin who's Armenian* and watched as he tried to get rid of me. Watched and learned.

Jirair isn't sure what to do, and so it's time for me to speak. Calmly, now. Don't show a thing.

"Your father told you the stories, Emin. He told you about what happened in Trebizond on the Black Sea coast, back in 1915. One day, the streets were filled with Turkish soldiers holding bayoneted rifles, who searched the Christian Armenian houses for weapons that did not exist. The town crier told the inhabitants that in four days all Armenians—there were about a thousand in Trebizond—would be evacuated for the duration of the Great War, and that any Muslim caught hiding an Armenian would be killed by hanging."

His grip on that briefcase is loosening. Slowly now. Down to a whisper.

"Your father was ten years old at the time of the march inland, and he told you that when people fell behind they were bayoneted and tossed into the river, which would wash them back out, past Trebizond, to the sea. The river was choked with bodies that had caught on branches, the stink of decomposition hovering over their long march. Your grandmother fell during that march, was stuck through with a bayonet and tossed into the water; four days later your grandfather was shot. Your father escaped from an internment camp in the desert, where the starving rolled in the sun, cut apart by dysentery, and made his way back to Trebizond, where he found an apartment picked clean by Turkish peasants. Even the linoleum had been ripped from the floors."

The surprise on Emin's face—wide-eyed, mouth gaping—is almost comical. Don't laugh. Don't smile.

"That wasn't the end, because your father and other stray boys were gathered and auctioned off to Muslim families so they could be converted to Islam. Again he escaped—which was lucky for him, because in the coming weeks even the converted Armenians were shipped off to their deaths."

Emin's face is apoplectic, shifting through emotions. All the power he's been trying to sustain leaves him quickly. Right. His eyes are wet, but he's not crying. Not yet. He says, "What are you, a spy?"

"That's exactly what I am," I tell him. "A spy into your soul."

Emin turns abruptly to Jirair. "Go."

Jirair leaves and will walk back to the corner where Libarid is sitting in terror. They will speak, but briefly, because Jirair wonders who I could be—*what* I could be—and Libarid will sympathize with his confusion. That's the nature of this. Confusion. With confused people you can do anything.

"Who are you working for?"

"For so many people, Emin. For Wilhelm Adler."

"Wilhelm? But he's . . ."

"He was never on your side. He works with Ludvík Mas, as do I. Remember that name. Ludvík Mas."

He dwells on that a moment, and it connects to a memory he has of an early girlfriend, Yeva, whose father sabotaged their relationship, turning the young lovers against one another. "You're here to ruin me," he says.

"Yes, I am."

He raises his gun to the side of my face, presses the cool barrel into my cheek.

Do it.

He won't do it yet. Shooting a woman is not what he's come here to do.

He must be forced.

"Yeva was a bitch. You know she was."

"What?"

Keep him confused. "I'm not scared of you. Yeva wasn't scared of you. No one is. Go ahead, pull the trigger. Your bullets can't hurt me."

This close, his face is coarse with all the sweat.

I spit into it.

He snaps back as if bitten, furious now. He's going to do it. I know he will. First he'll try to get answers wherever he can.

He steps back and snatches the radio handset. He's weeping now. "She told me," he says. "How did she know?"

"What did she say to you?" asks the radio.

"They're lying," I say quietly. "They know me."

He peers through teary eyes at me as he speaks into the radio. "Just that . . . that . . ." He raises the pistol.

A gunshot.

But not his.

Another pistol, from beyond the door.

No.

I grit my teeth as the numbers fall apart and then line up again.

Emin's head jerks around. He squeezes the handle of his brief-case.

Out there among the passengers. Could only be Ádám, my guard, or—

Childhood in Turkey. Slaughter by troops. Family on the run, then landing in a strange country with nothing to their name. Hatred grown old over the years and replaced by pragmatism. Pragmatism gives way to disappointment— where is the tough young man now? So he leaves the family, looking for that youth, and is put in the middle of a situation where he can rediscover that tough, angry young man.

Libarid.

I was wrong.

Another gunshot, and then the plane shifts, the floor tilts, I fall back—

I never saw this.

Gripping the suitcase detonator, he reaches for the door.

Which opens before he can touch it.

Libarid. You idiot.

But I'm the one who lost track. *I'm* the one with the bad wiring. Now I know.

And in that final instant I show him with my face that this was not how it was supposed to be.

Emin's hand seizes up, thumb on the button.

KATJA

•

For a week I do not return. I stay in a coastal village east of Kilimli in a small pension that doesn't bother asking for papers. Each night a heavy woman with dark hair on her upper lip brings my hot water in a pail for washing, and that first night I use it to clean Stanislav's knife. Afterward I sit on the terrace wrapped in a towel, watching the Black Sea, which my hostess calls the *Karadeniz*, disappear into the night.

I sleep late and in the early afternoon drink tea in a café near the water. The proprietor, a thin man with sun-blackened skin, greets me personally by my second visit, then tells me in English about the trips I should take to Turkey's many natural wonders. I understand little, but his English is musical, and his animated face is as absorbing as the sea. His monologues help me maintain my calm.

Afterward I walk the shore but don't swim. Fishermen at the small dock watch me pass as they mend their nets, but they never speak to me, which is something I appreciate.

Here I eat what they eat, sea bass encrusted in salt. I drink their hot black tea with milk from glasses that singe my fingers and

twice speak Russian with the café proprietor's daughter, a litera-
ture student in Ankara. She has big dark eyes I'm envious of.

"You don't have a man with you?"

I shake my head. "But I'm married."

"And you came to Turkey alone?"

"I needed to get away."

She scratches the corner of her lip with a long fingernail. "You
are a progressive, *da?*"

I shrug.

"I am a progressive," she says, smiling. "I make my father crazy.
He says I act like a man. He even calls me 'son'!"

I look at the proprietor washing glasses.

His daughter says, "You like it here?"

"It's very restful."

"It's very boring. This is not the real world. The real world is in
the capital. Here . . . it's like where you go when you want to die a
peaceful death."

I smile at her, then wave to her father for another black tea.

On Saturday, the tenth of May, I check out of the pension,
thank the mustached woman, and say good-bye to the father and
daughter at the café. Then I'm on the train.

During my week away, Istanbul has changed. It's gotten
brighter, the colors more vivid, the voices a higher pitch. I've still
got plenty of Deutschmarks, but I'm afraid that if I go to the Pera
Palas I'll run into that man I slept with, whose name I've lost
track of.

So I check into the dark but cheap Sultan Inn and take a nap
on the small bed until evening, when I wash and go out.

It's inevitable that I'll return—it's the old Militia cliché: A
criminal always returns to the scene of the crime. So I find myself

again in the lobby of the Hotel Erboy, where I struggled with the English in the *Herald Tribune* before following Peter Husák up to his room. I pick up another copy.

A desk clerk smiles at me as I pass him on my way to the elevator, which takes me to the fifth floor and a set of stairs leading to a small rooftop bar and restaurant half full of foreigners sipping drinks and stretching tired legs. I climb onto a stool and order *rakı*. The bartender, a small, efficient man, produces it quickly, alongside a dish of mixed nuts.

Here is a surprise. From the front page of the newspaper, General Secretary Tomiak Pankov glares back at me like a stern father. The headline tells me that he vehemently denies charges of funding terrorists leveled at him by a Swedish law-enforcement officer more than a week ago at an Interpol conference here in Istanbul.

That conference. The one Libarid never made it to.

Socialism, says our great leader, *has no need of violence or subterfuge. It is recognized by all the world as our only hope for peace and the salvation of our natural environment.*

I fold the paper, unsure whether I should smile at that. And I know then what that hesitation is—it's the weight of knowing that I'll soon be returning home. As if to remind me, a melancholy prayer begins from the glowing minarets of the Aya Sofia.

Behind me are small tables filled with strangers whom I, in my naïveté, assume are simple, only because I don't know their secrets. And to them, I'm a simple face at the bar, nothing more.

Then I spot a face I know, and the surprise almost makes me drop my glass. My first impulse is to flee, but I've grown to hate my impulses. So I take my glass over to a table at the edge, where a handsome man is staring morosely into his beer, ignoring the vista of nighttime Istanbul.

"Hello, Gavra."

He hasn't shaved in a few days. His pink eyes show he's been crying, and I wish I hadn't disturbed him. He stands, hands flailing at his sides. "Katja." His lips work the air a moment. "What are you—"

"May I?"

"Of course." He waves at the other seat and settles back down.

"I'm on vacation," I say.

He nods, but he looks very confused. "Me, too."

"Are you all right?"

Gavra takes a drink, then wipes his mouth with the back of his hand as the muezzin's prayer continues. "Not really."

"Can I help?"

He shakes his head. "I'll survive."

For a while we only drink and he smokes, both of us looking everywhere except at one another. Then I bring up something I think will be easy for us to discuss. "Did you and Brano ever figure out that hijacking?"

He continues to not look at me, but I can see tears returning. "We'll never figure it out."

"And Adrian Martrich?"

Gavra's taken by a sudden coughing fit, so I can barely make out his answer: "He's dead."

I don't ask how Adrian died, because the fact is I'm not even interested. People die every day, and the life I led a long time ago, before killing Peter Husák—the life I'll soon return to—carries no weight for me now. It will soon, but not yet, and I like this disconnection.

Once he's recovered, he wipes his eyes and says, "I don't know what to believe anymore."

"What do you mean?"

He doesn't answer. Instead, he puts his hand on mine and squeezes. Although I've always been fond of Gavra, this touch disturbs me in a way I can't quite place. Perhaps because the prayer is finished, and we're in silence. I find myself thinking that, if all I had to worry about was solving some damned case, I'd be skipping by now. He says, with surprising conviction, "Katja, I just want to be home again."

I smile, as if I understand.